JAKE ISTENHEGYI

THE ACCIDENTAL DETECTIVE

Nikki Nelson-Hicks

Third Crow Press

Third Crow Publishing
Gallatin, TN 37066
www.nikkinelsonhicks@gmail.com

Publisher's Note: This is a work of fiction. Names, characters, places, and incidents are a product of the author's imagination. Locales and public names are sometimes used for atmospheric purposes. Any resemblance to actual people, living or dead, or to businesses, companies, events, institutions, or locales is completely coincidental.

Book Layout © 2016 BookDesignTemplates.com
Cover art by Jeffrey Hayes, www.plasmafiregraphics.com

ISBN 978-1-7320967-9-0

CONTENTS

A quick word to the Reader:

Hello there!

I wanted to say something to the readers of the earlier versions of the Jake Istenhegyi stories-

THANK YOU. (hugs and socially distanced kisses)

And a quick explanation of why I went back and revisited stories that came out way back in 2016.

When I was asked to write the first story, "A Chick and Dick and A Witch Walk into a Barn", it was supposed to be a one shot. A 1500-word story to be published in an anthology called Poultry Pulp (pulp stories with chickens as a central theme). The anthology never saw the light of day, but my story impressed the editor enough that he asked if I wanted to do an entire Jake Istenhegyi, The Accidental Detective series. And, as I have often responded to opportunities that would have such a huge impact on my life, I said, "Ok, sure. What the hell. Might be fun."

I finished the last story, "Corpses, Coins, Ghosts and Goodbyes", in 2018 and I thought that would be the end.

And then the Pandemic hit. With time on my hands, I revisited the first Jake story.

I thought, *"Holy shit. This is terrible. It has a good skeleton, but this story needs more meat on the bones."*

Jake, Bear, Mama Effie and the Odyssey Shop crew deserved better. Especially considering the hell I put them through.

I hope you agree.

Nikki Nelson-Hicks, August 2020

JAKE ISTENHEGYI:

THE ACCIDENTAL DETECTIVE

Book One

A Chick, a Dick, and a Witch Walk into a Barn

Bwack-Brains!
2020

For Tommy, who gave me my first chance.

CHAPTER ONE

The Shed

I'm screwed.

I am leaning against a splintered wall. My foot is the only thing holding the door shut against a horde of screaming demons slamming against it, cracks splintering in the thin veneer of wood.

Shit.

So, this is me. Jake Istenhegyi.

It's a hell of a way to spend my last birthday.

CHAPTER TWO

One Day Earlier...

New Orleans in July.

Not my favorite place to be.

The air was thick with sweat and everyone's temper was rising along with the mercury in the thermometer. A luckier man would spend such a day out on a veranda, sipping a cold drink, savoring the ice as it tapped against his teeth. Drinking it quickly just so he could get another one down just as fast.

But that lucky son of a bitch wasn't me.

No, I was underneath a desk, sweat dripping in my eyes, while I scraped off gray lumps of dried chewing gum.

"Disgusting...I swear, the next time I see him...son of bi-OW!" A sharp kick in my side stopped my revelries and I pulled out to see my assailant was indeed the son of a bitch in question.

Looming over me was my tenant/partner/best friend Barrington "Bear" Gunn.

A decorated veteran of the Great War, Gunn was a giant at six foot four with a square jaw that his face used as a shelf. Because of his size, many people passed him off as a goon but one look into his soft brown eyes, you would see why the ladies called him Bear.

I don't know what the War was like for young Barrington Gunn; he never spoke about it. I always imagined that he made a promise to himself in a muddy, bloody trench that if he survived, he would live the life of his dime novel heroes.

Because that's exactly what he did.

The second his feet touched American soil and without a dime in his pocket, he started up a private detective business, Gunn Detective Agency. Currently, he ran it out of a second-floor apartment of a building I own on Market Street. In polite circles, that would make me his landlord, but I'd be a damn fool to push that title.

Since he rarely had money and bartered his detective skills doing jobs for Mama Effie and letting me tag on. I like to think of myself as a detective apprentice, but I'm not sure if Bear would agree. I know Mama Effie would laugh at the idea. To them, I'm more lackey than Watson, would be my guess.

Bear held out his hand and pulled me off the floor like a ragdoll. "What the hell are you doing under my desk, Jake?"

"Cleaning up your mess, as usual. Mama Effie has been crawling up my ass all morning. You've got to stop stashing your old gum under the furniture. She's threatening to evict you for health code violations."

Bear grinned and tossed his fedora on the desk. "Who do I pay rent to? You or Mama Effie? You really need to assert yourself more, boy."

"Assert myself? I'm lucky I've kept my balls in my pants for as long as I have. Look, it might say Istenhegyi on the deed, but we all know who really runs this joint. I'm only here because Uncle Andor died and my father needed someone to watch over his investments. Investment! I doubt he's even seen this wreck firsthand." I felt my face flush red, my Hungarian pallor never failed to broadcast my emotions. "Don't even get me started."

"Calm down, Bela."

"I'm don't sound like...oh, never mind." I regretted the day we went to that double creature feature with Boris Karloff and Bela Lugosi. Ever since, Bear never missed a chance to make fun of my accent, as slight as it is. I spent most of my youth in boarding schools in Italy and France, for Chrissakes!

I tossed the scraper aside and sat in the chair across from him. "So, where have you been all morning?"

"Getting clients, buddy-boy." He tapped a shoebox sized package in his lap. "I got a call from Postmaster Klaus. This was waiting for me."

"What is it?"

"I dunno. It's a mystery." He pulled off the brown wrapping and tossed it aside. "Luckily, I'm in the mystery business."

I picked up the paper and read the return to address. "Idaho? Who do you know in Idaho?"

He shrugged and opened the box. Inside was a white envelope attached to a typewritten letter laying on top of several handwritten ones. He fanned them and a strong smell of roses filled the air.

"Love letters?" I asked.

He tossed the pile of letters on the desk and opened the envelope. A cascade of money flowed out.

I picked up the bills and counted. "There's over a hundred dollars here, Bear. What do they want you to do? Kill somebody?"

"Shh, I'm working." He chewed on his thumbnail as he read the letter. "Huh. Says here a kid by the name of Isaac Stiegerson moved down here to New Orleans two months ago to hitch up with a lonely heart pen pal. His family hasn't heard a word from him since. They want me to look in on it."

"You mean us."

"No, this is a solo job. Our lovebirds are shacking up in the bayou. I know how you prefer the feel of concrete beneath your feet."

That was true. Bear relished the dirtier side of the business. Stake outs, guns, and fistfights were Bear's world. Me? I preferred a Parisian café with beignets, linen napkins, and a newspaper. As far as I was concerned, anything beyond the city of New Orleans was marked 'here be dragons.'

Bear picked up his hat, folded the letter and put it in his coat pocket. "Daylight is wasting. I'd better get going."

"Shouldn't you read these letters? Get a better sense of what you are going up against?"

"I know all I need to know. Some dumbass farm boy gets himself a taste of Creole ass and now Daddy Warbucks wants his boy back home before some color gets added to the bloodline. It's a tale as old as time. If you want to play librarian and stink up your hands with that cheap toiletwater, be my guest." He opened the door. "By the way, can I use your car, Jake?"

I felt a chill go down my spine. My Kicsem, my darling, was a '32 Phaeton, hunter green exterior and deep red interior. I loved that car with my heart and soul.

"Didn't you buy a secondhand Ford last week?"

"About that. No." Bear knocked on the door frame. "Cash flow problems."

"Why not? You had the money." I felt my skin start to flush again. "I know because you borrowed it from me."

"Yeah...sorry. I ran into some old buddies. They invited me to a friendly game of cards and, well, it didn't end up so friendly."

"Goddammit, Bear."

"Look, I can pay you back." He held up the cash. "I bet I can squeeze more out of this old guy if I string him along enough. Come on, Jake. I can't work without a car. And we're partners, right?"

"Jesus, fine. Take her. Just promise me that you will take care of her."

Bear rolled his eyes, kissed his fingertips, and crossed his heart. "I promise. I will guard your precious Kicsem with my life."

When I tossed him the keys, I felt a little part of me peel away.

"I'll bring her back in the morning with a full tank of gas, okay? Oh, and that reminds me. Don't think I haven't forgotten about tomorrow."

Bear rummaged in his coat pocket and tossed a silver Zippo lighter. "Consider it an early birthday present."

"Thanks." A buxom blonde graced the front. She was fighting the wind over her skirt and losing much to my delight. I flicked it open and closed, bisecting her. "Maybe I'll take up smoking."

"About time! Jesus, by your age, I'd been smoking for over a decade! I have a big day planned for us, kid. First, breakfast of biscuits and gravy and thick, greasy slabs of fatty bacon at the Sun Coffee Shop, then a double feature of Cagney in *G Men* and Tracy in *The Murder Man* and a big fried chicken dinner over at Russo's. To top it all off, I am setting you up with the sweetest skirt in town, Edie."

"Edie? The girl at the dry cleaners? I can't get her to give me the time of day."

"She owes me a favor." He clicked his tongue and winked. "You and me, Jake. Tomorrow, we're gonna burn this damn town down!"

The frame rattled as he slammed the door behind him. That was Bear. His exits were just as loud as his entrances.

I scooped up the letters and read them.

I didn't glean much except that they were love letters, very explicit ones in fact, from a Henrietta Harleux to someone she called her 'Blond Stallion Beau'. Reading her responses to his letters was like hearing only one side of a conversation. Frustrating. If she came through with only half of the things she promised to do to young Mr. Stiegerson, he was one lucky son of a bitch.

New Orleans was drowning in luckier sons of bitches than me.

That night I dreamt of beautiful Creole women whispering wet promises and deep, dark kisses.

CHAPTER THREE

Power in the Blood

I woke up with rosewater-soaked letters spread around me like petals on an altar. The sweet smell clung in my nose and made my head pound like a hangover.

There was an irritating tap-tap-tapping at my door. It reminded me of the timid nuns at St. Bart's boarding school in Italy, the memories of which added fuel to my already throbbing head.

"WHAT!?!" I shouted at the door.

The tapping stopped and a small voice answered, "Mama Effie sent me to fetch you, sir."

The voice belonged to Mikey, a kid Mama Effie hired to do odd jobs around the Odyssey Shop, a junk store that took up most of the first floor. She ruled that space like a Queen, with a court of thugs that sat in velvet chairs, waiting for her commands. I don't know what sort of commerce the Odyssey Shop dealt in and I was smart enough not to inquire.

"What does she want?"

"I don't know but she's in a mood, sir. She gave me a firecracker and told me to set it off under your ass if you weren't awake."

"Oh, yeah?"

"But the door was locked, sir."

"Looks like it's my lucky day."

"Don't tell her I told you that, sir."

"You have my word, Mikey. Tell her Highness that I'll be right down."

"Yes, sir," he said and the sound of his bare feet slapping on the wooden floors echoed behind him.

My apartment is on the third floor, high above the stink so prevalent in New Orleans. I have crammed all of my earthly goods into three hundred square feet alongside a twin sized bed with thin mattress, a kitchenette with space for a hot plate, toaster and percolator (although only one can be plugged in at a time or the fuse box blows), and what Mama Effie describes as a combination private toilet/bath; I basically piss in the shower. Other calls of nature are answered in the loo downstairs. Mama Effie told me that these gratuities made my apartment a 'master suite' and I should feel grateful.

I've been here for five years. The only thing I feel is trapped.

I laid there for a few more minutes, rubbing my forehead to quiet the aching behind my eyes. I sat up and the letters fell to the floor around my feet. I grinned at the memory of Henrietta Harleaux and her Blonde Stallion Beau.

That lucky bastard.

Then I thought of Bear. I didn't hear him come home last night.

Am I the only unlucky bastard around here?

I picked out a pair of tan gabardine slacks and an undershirt from a pile on the floor. I took a quick sniff and figured there was still a day left before I had to make the decision to either wash or burn then. It didn't make sense to put on clean clothes since I was already on Mama Effie's shit list.

On the second floor, I stopped at Bear's office. He had a door installed with a frosted glass window emblazoned with his logo, *GUNN DETECTIVE AGENCY, Barrington Gunn, Esquire.* I doubt that he had a law degree. I suspect he just thought it sounded more professional than 'Barrington Gunn, Professional Snoop'.

I paused with my knuckles over the glass.

You want me to assert myself, old man?

I turned the door handle and opened the door.

"Bear?"

The room was dark, empty. More than just that. There was a void here. A weird chill ran up my spine. My Roma blood prickled causing the puckered scars on the back of my neck to start burning.

I've had them for as long as I can remember, these weird circular marks on the back of my neck. I was told by my Grandmother, a loveless old hag that could barely stand to look at her bastard half-Gypsy grandson, that they were a mark of sin. "That woman put them on you," she said. 'That Woman' was how the Istenhegyis referred to my mother; I never knew her name.

What I did know was that when they burned, something bad was about to happen.

Where are you, Bear?

There was a tug at my shirt.

"Jesus!" I held back from swinging my fist wildly into the wide-eyed face of Mikey.

"Sir, she's waiting. *And she's in a mood,*" he added in a whisper.

"Great. This day is just getting better and better."

****

I stood at the top of the stairs and looked down into the court of Mama Effie.

The first day we met, she blocked the door of the Odyssey Shop and stared me down. She was wearing a red and purple caftan with a turban covered in feathers that seemed alive in the breeze. The woman was stick thin, all sharp angles from her cheekbones down to her shins. In heels, she stood three inches taller than all 5'8" of me but, the way she looked down on me, so imperial and judging, it felt like three feet.

"So, you're Mr. Andor's nephew?" she said, her voice clipped and icy. She was a proud Creole that could count her family back to five generations. "The boy who comes all the way from overseas to claim his inheritance?"

"Yes, ma'am. I'm Janos Istenhegyi." I smiled and put my hand out to take hers. She looked at it for a second and then gave me a slack handshake. "And who do I have the pleasure of meeting?"

"I am Mama Effie. I take care of things." She looked me up and down, never once moving out of the doorway.

"I see."

"Do you? Really? So, you think you going to come here, out of nowhere, not knowing a thing, and start taking *care* of things?"

I straightened my shoulders and looked her dead in the eye. She cocked her head and waited. There was only one answer any smart twenty-year-old kid right off the boat could give.

"No?"

"Good boy." She smiled and slapped my cheek. Gently but with enough force to let me know what it could've been. "I think we're going to work together just fine, sweet boy."

That was Mama Effie.

And five years later, she was still taking care of things.

What those things were, I didn't ask for specific details.

The Odyssey Shop took up the entire first floor. A winding snake of shelves meandered throughout each stacked with knick-knacks, moldy books, empty mason jars and a thousand things I don't know the names for. On the grimy window was inscribed "We Go to the Ends of the Earth to Satisfy Your Needs!"

But I had yet to see a customer come through the door.

In the center of the room, Mama Effie kept court.

She was surrounded on four sides by waist high wooden walls. She sat on her throne with her cash box and ledger always at the ready.

Across from her, two large men stuffed into suits sat in high back winged chairs, sipping coffee, reading the paper, and waiting orders.

A short man in a porkpie hat with a sharp face like a rat stood at the railings. Mama Effie stuffed an envelope full and wrote on the outside. She closed it shut with a wax seal and handed it to the Rat Man. He tipped his hat and scurried off.

Like I said, I never asked specific details.

When the door shut, I felt her eyes lock on me.

"You going to come down here, Boy?" she said, pointing a long, lacquered finger to the floor. "Or do I need to send one of my men to carry you down?"

I didn't answer; I wasn't going to give her the satisfaction. I made my way down the stairs and over to her.

"Mikey said you wanted me?"

A finger went to her nose. "Boy, you smell like you fell into a whore's bath."

"It's a case. Bear and I are working on." Words stumbled from my mouth. I shook my head and tried to gain ground. "Look, what do you want? I'm busy."

I felt the goons behind me bristle. Mama Effie gave an almost imperceptible shake of her head and I felt the wave of hostility ease down.

"Well, now, let's get to business, then. So, you and Mr. Gunn are working a case, is that right? Isn't that an amazing coincidence because the little matter I need to discuss with you also concerns business with Mr. Gunn."

She pulled out a ragged piece of paper.

"This morning, three young men approached this establishment with an I.O.U. for gambling debts that they said were accrued by Mr. Barrington Gunn. According to this slip of whiskey stained paper, the debt would be erased by a Mr. Janos Istenhegyi, owner of the Odyssey Shop. Would you care to explain to me why I had to dip into the store's funds to pay off your friend's debts?"

I looked at the ragged piece of paper. My name was scrawled on the bottom in what I knew to be Bear's handwriting.

"That son of a bitch."

"That might be but I don't particularly care about his parentage. What I do care about is recompense."

"Don't worry. I- we can cover this. Bear was paid just yesterday for the case we're working."

"Really? Flush with cash, is he?"

"He's got rent covered for a year, if he doesn't blow it."

"Oh, well, I do like the sound of that." A sly grin crossed her face. "What sort of case are you two working?"

"Some farm boy started up a pen pal romance with a girl in the bayou. Bear went to go to talk to her and sort it out. Henrietta Harleaux."

Mama Effie sat taller, like a cobra ready to strike.

"Henrietta Harleaux? Is that who you are doing business with?"

"Why? Do you know her?"

"I know of her just as I am confident that she knows of me. More importantly, I know the snakes that surrounds herself with." She tapped her long nails on the counter. "Has Mr. Gunn returned?"

"No."

Mama Effie shook her head and tsked. "That is not good."

I rubbed the round scars on the back of my neck. "I checked in his office. I have a weird feeling…"

Mama Effie's long arm shot out, grabbed my shirt, and pulled me in closer. I felt like I was going to drown in her eyes. Everything around her swirled into nothing until there was only her and those beautiful eyes.

"There is power in your blood!" She hissed. "You'd best listen to it. Gunn is in dark trouble. You need to go to him."

She pushed me away and I felt myself waver a tiny bit as the room suddenly shifted into stark focus.

"Ok…ok…" I stumbled towards the door.

"Go and shower. You smell like a whore's den. Put on some fresh clothes. Make yourself presentable. But first," commanded Mama Effie, holding out her slender hand. "You'd better settle your tab. There's a good chance you're gonna die out there, Boy!"

CHAPTER FOUR

Bumpy Ride

I barely remember showering and putting on fresh clothes. It's a blur. The only thing that pushed me forward was the terrible feeling that I was already a dollar short and an hour too late.

I ran down the stairs and rushed to the door before I realized, "Damn! Bear took my car."

Mama Effie didn't even look up from her ledger. "I called for a cab. It is waiting for you outside."

"What? Ok, thanks," I said, baffled at her generosity. "I appreciate that."

She waved me away, "I'll start up a new tab."

The ground suddenly felt solid beneath my feet. That was the Mama Effie I knew.

Outside the Odyssey Shop, there was a Studebaker with yellow siding waiting for me. I got in the back seat and the driver took off.

"Where to?" asked the driver. All I could see was the back of his head and the triple fold of skin that rode on top of his starched white collar. I looked in the rearview mirror and saw pale blue eyes looking back at me.

I rattled off the address from the box Bear received yesterday.

"What do you want out there?"

"I need to find someone. Henrietta Harleaux. Heard of her?"

The cabbie pulled over hard enough to push me back into my seat. He parked the car and turned his massive bulk towards me.

"Look, I don't owe those bastards back there enough to get in the middle of a catfight between those two witches. Get out!"

"It's an emergency!"

"Not my concern, buddy. If you want me to put my ass on the line, I'm going to need some green, hear me?"

"I don't have time to argue with you. How much?"

"A Lincoln."

"Five dollars? That's highway robbery!"

He folded his arms over his thick gut. "Not my problem. Pay me or get out and start walking."

I pulled out my wallet and made a mental note to add this to Bear's running tab.

"Take it."

The cabbie sniffed the bill and stuffed it in his pocket.

"Hold on, buddy, this is gonna be a bumpy ride."

My fingers slipped around the lighter Bear had given me the day before. I doubt he bought it; more than likely found it laying on a table, unattended, and quickly appropriated. That is a term Bear used instead of 'stealing'. "It's what we used to say in the military. We don't steal. We appropriate items to serve a more useful purpose."

I flipped it open and closed, absently bisecting the blonde beauty, over and over again.

I wasn't paying any attention to where the driver was headed. My mind was too full of questions that rattled around in my brain. They flickered through with every flick of the lighter.

Who was Henrietta Harleaux?

flick

Why did Mama Effie react like that?

flick

What the hell kind of dark trouble was Bear mixed up in and, most importantly, what the hell was he pulling me into?

The skin around my temples felt tight. This wasn't getting me anywhere, so I closed the lighter and slid it in my pocket.

"So, tell me," said the driver. "What does that old witch got on you? You can tell me."

I shook my head. "Who? Mama Effie? For your information, I'm the owner, not her." I felt a bit of machismo crawl up my spine. "I'm the boss."

"Oh? Is that right? You Andor's boy? Damn shame about him. Fell under a bus, right?"

"His nephew, actually."

"I liked Andor. That old man knew how to throw a party. I gotta say I am surprised to know that the Odyssey Shop is still in the family. Scuttlebutt I heard was that Old Man Andor was drowning in debt, owed his ass hairs to some really shady folks and he was selling to cover what he owed. Well, until the bus took him out first."

"It was a damn shame," I said. I didn't know much about my uncle. The only time I ever heard my father say his brother's name, it was prefixed with that "Goddamn Pervert" so I doubt the world felt a great loss when the wheels crushed the old man's head.

I pulled my fedora down over my eyes and settled into the seat. "I'm going to catch some winks. Let me know when we get there."

"For another slice, I'll even sing you a lullabye."

"Shut up and drive."

CHAPTER FIVE

Swamp Beavers

I fell asleep quickly but the dreams I had did nothing to help me rest. Maybe it was the bumpy road but I dreamt I was on a ship that was being tossed around in a hurricane. I fought with the wheel, the sea spray stinging my eyes. I didn't know where I was going but I knew in my gut I needed to get there fast. All the time I was fighting against the ocean, I could hear a woman's laughter just above the crashing waves.

The driver honked his horn twice, waking me from my nautical adventure.

"Wake up, Sunshine."

I tipped my fedora off my eyes. All around us were deep, lush trees. What passed for a paved road continued ahead of us.

"Where the hell are we?"

"This is as far as your fiver goes, buddy. I'm not going any closer to Harleaux than I need to." He turned his enormous bulk around to face me. "Look, I don't you from Adam but you seem to be a good guy. Are you sure you want to get yourself messed up in all of…" He waved his meaty hands around. "That?"

I wiped the sleep out of my eyes; I still felt seasick from the dream. The deep green around me looked impenetrable. Heat from outside was steaming up the windows.

Jesus, what the hell am I doing out here?

In our little tag team of Detective and Sidekick, Bear was the one who jumped into the dirt and muck with both feet. He loved the rough and ready side of the business. He'd come back to the office with a busted lip on one than more occasion. "Just part of the business," he'd say and spit blood into the sink.

Me? No, thank you, very much. That was not my idea of any sort of business I'd want to be a part. I was the idea guy. I did the research. I'd ask questions, interview people; I was the one with the soft touch. "You got the Face, Jake," Bear would say. "I got the fists."

Shit, Bear. What did you drag us into?

"Yeah," I said, releasing a deep breath I didn't even realize I was holding. "Yeah, this is something I have to do."

"All right. It's your funeral. There's a path other there to the left. Follow it and you'll eventually find a road that leads to her cottage. Oh," he reached forward and pulled a business card out from glove box and gave it to me. "The name is Moe Shrevey. Call me. That is, if you make it out in one piece."

I tucked his card in my jacket pocket. "Thanks. I don't suppose I could convince you to wait for me?"

"Wait??" Moe laughed so hard I thought he might choke. "You don't have enough Lincolns to keep me out here! Now, git. I got other rides."

I closed the door, took a step away and heard him whistle.

"Oy! By the way, watch out for the gators, they are sneaky bastards. They'll slip up on you and pull you under before you know what bit you. Oh! And keep an eye out for swamp beavers."

"I'm sorry…. swamp what?"

I could hear his laughter on the thick swampy air as he drove away.

Bear, you owe me big.

CHAPTER SIX

Follow the Bird

Back when my life made sense, I spent my time in the best salons and cafes in Paris. During the day, we'd sleep until the sun went down and then we'd meet up to drink and talk about the news of the day. I was surrounded by some of the best minds of Europe. Or at least that's what we told ourselves when the absinthe kicked in.

God, that feels like a lifetime ago.

I remember listening to two of my friends arguing about a hotly contested theory that all life on Earth started in a hot soupy mess. Luc argued, "That's insane, Rene. Look around you! Are you trying to tell me, that all of this started in a bubbling puddle of mud?"

Rene read a from a textbook he'd stolen from his ex-girlfriend to defend his argument, but we were too young and too drunk to listen.

Now, as I pull my foot out of the soupy mess that passes for ground out here in the godforsaken bayou of Louisiana, all I can offer up is a sad, "You were right, Rene. I owe you one."

For the thousandth time, I wondered why anyone in their right mind would leave the comforts of New Orleans for this swampy hell? Or even Idaho?

The trail that Moe told me to follow led me deeper into the bayou. I removed my hat and wiped my brow with my sleeve. I felt dizzy from the heat and from the cacophony that came from all around. The only thing that kept me moving forward was the ominous sounds that twittered from above me in the trees and the menacing clicking sounds that came from the tall clumps of weeds in the swamp.

click-clack...click-clack

Swamp beavers?

The strange click clacking was coming closer. I stopped. A cold rush of fear ran through me as I realized I didn't have anything to protect myself. I never carried a gun; that was Bear's style.

I saw a stick as round as my arm on the ground to my left. I held it high, ready to smash whatever was coming at me.

click-clack....click....bwwwack...

Wait....what?

The tension in my shoulders lessened as a solid white chicken calmly stepped from the weeds.

"Jesus."

The chicken cocked its head and looked at me with a serious glare. It didn't seem to be any more impressed with me than I was with it. It turned and went back from where it came.

I decided to follow it. Perhaps it belonged to Henrietta Harleaux? Or someone who would know how to find her? What did I have to lose?

I would lose sight of the bird for a few moments only to have it suddenly emerge from a bush, poke a head out, cluck, and forge ahead. It was as if it wanted me to follow it.

In hindsight, maybe it was.

The trail ended at a out of place hedgerow. I'm not a botanist but it reminded me of a Hawthorn hedge that lined the Istenhegyi estate in Budapest. Thick, rough woody roots that looked like gnarled fists held up a green gate of barbed vines. Impassable unless you wanted to come out the other side looking like a tic tac toe board of scratches. It seemed to go on and on for miles.

The chicken scratched the ground, clucked and dodged its way through the hedge.

Damn!

"Silly girl! Where are you been?" I heard a woman say beyond the hedge. "You nearly missed suppertime."

"Hello!" I shouted.

There was a pause. "Who did you bring this time, Hester? Silly chicken. Hello! Can I help you?"

"Yes! I hope so. My name is Jake Istenhegyi. I'm looking for Henrietta Harleaux. Could you tell me if I am on the right road?"

"Oui! Ah, you are a naughty girl, Hester." I heard the chicken squawk as she put the bird down. "You are very close, sir. I am she."

"Excellent. That makes for one problem solved. Now, for my most obvious one: how do I get through his hedgerow?"

"I don't normally entertain strangers but," she laughed softly. "I'll make an exception. Walk a dozen steps to your left. You will find a door. I'll be waiting for you there."

"Is there? I could've sworn," I muttered as I counted my steps.

10..11....12.

"I'll be damned."

There was a round wooden door carved into a deep dark frame that bled into the curly hedgerow.

I opened the door.

On the other side was a woman so beautiful my tongue automatically stuck to the roof of my mouth.

Mocha creamy skin, wavy black hair that rolled down her back, and pale green eyes flecked with gold. She was impossible. I suddenly understood why young Master Stiegerson would leave the green fields of Idaho for the swampy bayou. No farmer's daughter could compete with this goddess that stood before me. She was wearing a simple, cornflower blue housedress but there was nothing simple about the figure underneath that fabric.

"You are staring," she said. A smile slid across her lips and she winked. "It's not very polite."

I felt my pale Hungarian skin flush red. I gave her a business card that Bear had printed up for me. "Forgive me. I blame the heat. My manners are not up to par. The cabbie, he left me stranded out there."

"Neither are mine now that you mention it," she said as she took a quick glance over the card and then deftly slipped into her ample cleavage. "I apologize. Let's get out of this sun. I have cold, sweet tea in my cottage. If you'd like some, please, follow me."

"Lead the way."

CHAPTER SEVEN

A Nasty Habit

We went a far bit down a dirt road that was well traveled. I cursed Moe silently in my head and wondered how well my own car fared on this bumpy road. Bear promised he'd bring her back with a full tank and I was going to keep him to it.

She had a Craftsman style bungalow that set back away from the road. Copper windchimes hung from the eaves and made sharp tinkling noises in the slight breeze. Honeysuckle vines crawled up the walls and the sweet smell mingled with jasmine planted around her doorstep. A huge oak loomed over the building providing shade. The branches curved and twisted like the strong arms of a lover protecting its prize. Spanish moss swayed from the oak like lace.

Further back, I could see what I assumed to be a shed and a barn. The ground was riddled with several rows of tire tracks that led towards the barn.

Dozens of chickens roamed around freely, ignoring the wooden fence that marked off the property. They were all different colors and sizes. They mainly kept away from us except, Hester, the white hen that had led me here, pecked at my shoe.

"She really does like you," said Harleaux as she approached her door. "Come inside. Any friend of Hester's is a friend of mine."

It was cooler inside. Comfortable, well lived in and soothing with the smell of lavender everywhere.

The walls were dotted with framed photographs of young men and women, several in graduation caps and gowns. On the mantle above the fireplace were two photographs. One of a man outside a law firm. The other of a young, beautiful woman, very heavy with child. Beside each frame were four white candles that had been recently burned. Postcards depicting saints leaned against their waxy pillars.

I motioned to the photographs on her wall. "Family?"

"Those are my sons."

"Your sons?"

"And those are my daughters. And that one," she pointed to the pregnant woman on the mantle. "is my granddaughter."

I couldn't keep the shock off my face.

She smiled at my distress at the question I dare not

ask a lady. She sat up straighter which merely impressed the bounty of her form and brushed back her dark, lush hair. "Thank you, Mr. Istenhegyi. I am very blessed."

"You should bottle up some of that blessing and take it to market, Mrs. Harleaux. You could make a fortune."

It was her turn to blush. She bowed her head in gratitude.

I pushed the envelope.

"I see a few college graduates in those photos. Expensive. How did you afford it…if you don't mind me asking?" My manners forced me to tack that on at the last minute.

Her eyebrows arched and for a moment, I was sure she as going to escort me out the door. She cleared her throat and said, "It is a valid question even if it is rude. But, I suppose it is simply a consequence of your vocation. If you must know, I make my way through this world by selling eggs and chickens to local culinary connoisseurs. My birds are fed a special blend that makes their meat especially tender and delicious."

"A secret ingredient?"

Her lips slid into a sly smile. "Generations old. In leaner times, I supply the locals with what I can to make ends meet."

It was my turn to arch a brow.

"Moonshine." She made a tutting sound with her tongue. "Don't be vulgar. Please, sit," she said. "Make yourself at home while I prepare some iced tea."

I sat down on a well cushioned loveseat and put my fedora on end table beside me. I wiped the back of my neck with my handkerchief.

She came back and placed the serving tray on the coffee table. She poured two glasses of deep brown sweet tea and handed me one. The coldness bit into my fingertips as I took it. I gulped it down like it was ambrosia.

She sat down in the chair across me from, tucking her long legs demurely beneath her. She deftly pulled my card from out of her blouse.

"Now, what can I do for you, Mr. Isten…"

"Istenhegy. Ishten-hedgey. It's a mouthful, I know."

"Not from around here, then?"

"Not originally. I'm from all sorts of places, hard to pin down just one spot. My family is Hungarian. Budapest. I moved here five years ago to take over my uncle's shop on Market Street."

"But the card says private investigator."

"Part time. I help my partner, Barrington Gunn,

when he needs me. He's the actual detective."

She poured me another glass. "And why are you here?"

I told her about the letter, Isaac Stiegerson. I decided to keep the part about Bear to myself for now.

"Oh, yes. Isaac. He did visit me but," she shook her head. "It was puppy love, nothing else. He was not ready for marriage. He left weeks ago. I do not know where."

"Ah, well. I have just one more question," I said as I put my empty glass on the end table.

"Non!" she cried out causing me to jerk and knock my fedora off the table. "Please, use the coaster."

"Excuse me," I said and bent down to retrieve my hat. I saw something on the underside of the table that made my heart stop.

A wad of gray chewing gum.

I put the glass on the coaster and carefully put my fedora next to me.

I smiled. I hoped my pale skin did not give away my game.

"I apologize," I said. "My grandmother would be so ashamed of my manners."

"No harm done," said Henrietta Harleaux, as she sat back in her chair. "Now, what else did you want to ask?"

One thing my father taught me was that a good attorney never asks a question that he doesn't already know the answer to. I decided to put that to the test.

"I'm concerned about my partner, Barrington Gunn. He said he was coming here to speak with you. He didn't return, work is piling up, and, worst of all, he took my car!" I shrugged with a laugh. "Have you seen him?"

Henrietta Harleaux looked square in the eye and never blinked.

"No."

I kept her gaze.

"Oh well!" I gave my best Gosh Darn grin as I stood to leave. "Maybe he took my car on some joyride. I wouldn't be surprised. Not the first time, that's for sure. Thank you for your time, Mrs. Harleaux. I'll see myself out."

"I'm sorry I couldn't be of more help,"

Before I made it to the door, she was in front of me, blocking my out way. The smell of lavender and sandalwood made my head swim.

"Mr. Istenhegyi," she said. "You can't leave yet."

My pulse quickened and I fought to keep my eyes flat as my mind raced.

"Why?"

"Don't you need to call a cab?" She waved a thin hand towards her telephone.

Smooth, Istenhegyi....cucumber cool. Idiot.

I fought to keep my voice light as I plastered a clueless smile on my face. "May I use your phone?"

CHAPTER EIGHT

The Barn

I gave a story about meeting the cab back at the main road where he let me off.

I walked down the road until I was sure she couldn't see me and circled back to her bungalow. Keeping low and away from the windows, I followed the tracks that led towards the barn.

Bear sat in that chair, chewing that vile gum he loved and, while she was in the kitchen getting their drinks, he wadded it up and....oh God...the tea.

I waited for any sign of poisoning but none came. I sighed deeply, feeling stupid but relieved at the same time. I wiped my forehead, trying to think. The air was hot, so hot it had a smell like thick, stagnant miasma. And the bugs. They swarmed around me, biting and just plain annoyed me. I couldn't concentrate. I swiped and scratched.

"Think, Janos. Think!" I said, slapping the mosquito biting my face. Janos is my birth name. Bear pestered me into changing my name to Jake but, in my heart, I was still Janos. "What do we know? What are the facts? He was there. Harleaux lied about that. But why? And where is he now? And where is my car?"

There wasn't much action coming from inside the house but, outside, the chickens were starting to become a real pest. Two of the feathered bastards ran up and pecked me on the ankle, drawing blood. I kicked those two only to have a half a dozen more trying to trip me. They followed me, clucking and pecking all the way. I finally decided to hell with stealth and started running towards the barn.

It was a typical English style barn, large, square and bulky. The roof looked swayback on one side, as if it were half done or falling in. The doors weren't locked, and I pulled them open, hitting a couple of chickens in the process. I admit, it was more in revenge than necessity.

I slammed the door behind me and leaned against it. I closed my eyes as I caught my breath.

Opening them, I knew how Gepetto felt inside the whale. The wooden planks and rafters arched upward like a grayish ribcage. The barn was empty except for hay strewn haphazardly on the floor and the chickens. God, there were dozens and dozens of the damn birds, scratching around on the floor, roosting up in the rafters, on the ribs of the roof and inside my car.

In less than 24 hours, the filthy birds had nested inside her, scratching up the upholstery and littering the floor with feathers, hay and muck. The outside was splattered with white offal. The excrement had etched tears into the paint as if it were acid.

Six chickens sat on the roof and stared down at me with an imperious silence. I swiped at them with my fedora.

"Get off of her, you stinking feather bags! Git!"

Five of the birds took flight, leaving one behind.

"You son of a bitch!" I opened the door to get a foothold and batted at the bird with my hat. "I said GIT!"

The bird ducked then, slowly, regally, crooked its head to the side. An enormous scarlet comb flopped to one side as it looked down on me with one golden red eye.

There was something other than chicken in that stare. It made the hairs on the back of my neck bristle. I took a step backwards… and my foot landed on something that squawked in anger. I twisted my back by doing a wild two-step as I barely kept my balance.

Turning, I saw dozens, hundreds of chickens now, flocking between the door and me.

"Oooookay. Good chickens. Nice chickens." I said, holding up my hands. "Sorry I stepped on your friend back there, couldn't be helped."

A low rumble came from behind me. It was like a big cat's purr, almost subsonic but loud enough I could feel it in my bones. The chickens stared up at something right over my shoulder and started to bop their heads in rhythm.

I followed their gaze back to the thing on the roof of my car. It was definitely no chicken. The monster was dancing, its wings outstretched and flapping. The scythe like talons on the end of its scaly legs ripped through the cloth roof. Its neck was ostrich- like, bald with feathers clinging to it in small clumps, as if someone had gripped its head and stretched it out. It undulated like a snake and the head lolled in rhythm with the swirling neck. Its beak was open with the tongue hanging to the side. Golden spittle dribbled off and puddled on the roof where it sizzled and bubbled.

Its eyes blazed in fury as it caught me watching its grotesque burlesque. It began to hiss and croak out a hellish crowing that the other chickens echoed back. The sheer volume made my ears feel like popping. I clapped my hands over my ears and kicked my way towards the door but with every two chickens, three would take their place.

Fine. New plan.

I ran back to my car, clearing a path with every kick.

The creature on the roof, growled and snapped at my hand as I pulled open the door but missed. I hopped into the driver seat to find the key was still in the steering column. Finally, something going my way! Maybe Fortuna would bless me once more...and I checked the glove box. Yes! Inside, I found Bear's loaded .38 with some spare bullets.

I pulled the toggle and the car started up with vengeance in her heart. My baby knew when she was being abused. I slammed my foot down on the gas and suddenly I was engulfed in a wave of frenzied chickens. Talons, claws, feathers and beaks was all I could see as a flock jumped up from the backseat. I beat at them with my free hand and tried to keep the car from swerving, but it was too much. In the chaos, I rammed the car into wall.

I pushed my way out of the car and slammed the door on the crazed chickens inside. Coming at me, hundreds of chickens were charging with the monster chicken was leading the way. I pulled out the .38 and took three shots at the horde. Nothing. A useless waste of bullets. I looked around the empty barn for a weapon, anything!

Beyond my crunched-up car, I spied something…a door.

As luck would have it, I had crashed not five feet from a door that led to…who knew? Who cared? As long as it got me away from this bloodthirsty flock of hellchickens, that was all I needed.

I climbed over my hood, rushed inside, and slammed the door, severing a few beaks and clawed feet in the process. I slid to the floor and tried to catch my breath. There wasn't a lock on the door, but I didn't think the damned beasties were clever enough to turn a handle. I looked around. It was a windowless room but well lit. There was a partition that ran halfway through the middle. The breeze felt good on my-

Wait. Breeze?

I looked up.

This just wasn't my day.

There was no ceiling. The room opened up to the sky. A dozen sleeping chickens roosted on the railing that boxed in the room.

"Sonofabitch!" I swore. The chickens above ruffled their feathers and settled back into their naps. To hell with them. I stood up and kicked the partition, hard. "SON OF A-"

"Mmmmmrgh." I heard a muffled grunt from behind the cheap plywood wall.

I readied the .38 and held my breath and I stole a look.

Oh, sweet merciful God….

My fist clenched.

I nearly wasted another bullet.

I found him.

I found Bear.

CHAPTER NINE

A Chick, A Dick, and a Witch Walk into a Barn…

On the floor, there was a red and black mosaic of a snake. Starting at the tip of the tail, my eyes followed it, round and round, as it encircled a pit. Covering the pit was a large wheel supported by a pillar I only imagined was rooted at the bottom of the pit.

On the wheel, strapped naked like a sick recreation of Da Vinci's Vitruvian Man was Bear.

"Istenem…" *Oh my God* rolled out in my mother tongue.

His stomach was flayed open. The skin flaps were carefully stitched to the sides so his guts were open like a buffet. His intestines were pock marked and torn where the chickens had gorged themselves on the tenderest bits of the banquet laid out before them. The air reeked of blood and shit. I pressed the back of my hand against my mouth to keep from tossing up my stomach.

He stared at me with one wild, rolling eye. The other socket was a red mess where the chickens had pecked out the eyeball. Bear's face was mutilated. His nose, cheeks and his ears were shredded. His lips were sewn shut.

"Oh, Christ…hold on, Bear…just…hold on."

My father always said a man always needed three things in his pockets: a handkerchief, a wallet and a sharp knife. I shoved the gun into my waistband and pulled out my pocketknife. "I'm here, Bear. Everything is going to be okay."

He shook his head violently. The wheel turned slightly. He snorted heavily, like a tortured bull. Clots of bloody snot blew out. He was terrified. I wasn't even sure he realized it was me.

"Bear, it's me. Jake Istenhegyi. Bear!" I held his face gingerly, what there was left of it, and forced him to focus on my face. "Listen to me. I'm going to get you out."

He shook his head and tears ran out of his one good eye.

I stroked his forehead and tried to calm him. "But you have to be still. Do you understand me? I need you to be still so I can cut the threads. Okay?"

I took his still silence as acceptance.

I started snapping the threads with my knife. I kept my blade sharp so it was easy work.

I wasn't prepared for what spilled out of his mouth. Salt. Bloody, pink and black clotted salt. Bear gagged up the rest of the foul stew and sputtered out something unintelligible.

I bent down closer to hear him. "What?"

His breath was hot and smelled like a burnt penny.

"Kill me, Jake." he whispered. "And run like hell."

"No...no! I can get you out, Bear." I started cutting the ropes that held him down. I freed one of his hands and started working on one around a leg.

He whimpered and tears flowed from his one eye. A long thin wail keened out from him; a horrible sound to come from the man I knew.

"Christ! I'm done for!" he cried, "It's no good....no good....."

"Shut up! I am not leaving you here!"

Cutting on the rope, I noticed something loosely tied to a spoke next to his leg. It was a bone. A tibia, if I wasn't mistaken. I poked at it with my knife. The bone fell away and into the pit below.

A horrible buzzing began to swell from below.

"Ohnoohnoohno...not again...NOT AGAIN!" Bear swung his free arm and beat himself in the head with his fist. I grabbed his arm to stop him.

The buzzing amplified, echoed up from the pit along with the smell of decay and sickness.

I leaned over to see what was making that horrible noise.

A thick flying black column of blue bottle flies rushed up and enveloped me. I fell back, kicking and swiping at the biting, flying bugs. Bear screamed as they ripped into his open wounds, burrowing in like fat, black ticks.

I dropped the knife and swung at the black cloud with my fedora as the cloud of flies buzzed at my head, kamikaze style. They were vicious. They spiral dived straight for my eyes, my mouth, my nose. Blinding me, suffocating me. I twirled like a howling dervish, all the while my friend screamed and bucked on the wheel, threatening to pitch it off the stake and send it down into the pit.

In the middle of this hell, a woman's laughter came from behind me.

I turned and opened one eye to a cat's eye slit. Henrietta Harleaux was standing next to the partition, calmly surveying the horror.

"Come back for more of my hospitality, Monsieur Istenhegyi?" She sauntered in, her beauty and grace out of place in such a sewer. She had slipped into a stunning white gown and turban. "Or did you see something else you liked?"

I went for the .38 with one hand and swiped at the biting flies that dived at my eyes with the other. Blinded, I pointed the gun in her general direction. "Keep... ack!" I coughed and gagged as a fly rushed into my mouth.

She laughed that high crystalline laugh drilled into my ears like an ice pick. "Poor boy." She raised one slender mocha hand and the flies lifted. She puckered her lips as if to whistle and blew a silent note. The black cloud swirled into a corkscrew, twisting and swirling above me and Bear. With a casual flick of her wrist, the cloud descended back into the pit.

"Nice trick." I said. I steadied my grip to stop my hand from shaking. "Now, it's my turn."

"Oh?" She cocked her head to the side, much like the feathered bastards that crowding around her. "How many tricks do you have, Mr. Istenhegyi?"

"Only one. I call it the 'saving my friend and getting the hell away from the crazy backwater bitch' trick. It's pretty new." I kept my gun on her as I bent down to pick up my knife. "I doubt you've heard of it."

She shook her head and took a step closer to me. "I don't think so." The chickens flowed in behind her like the train of a bridal gown. "I need him. This month has been difficult."

"Stay back!"

She shook her head and smiled.

"Stop. I will shoot!"

She threw her arms open and stepped up the pace.

"Ha! You can't hurt me!"

She was five feet away.

Dammit.

"Stop!"

Three feet.

"Dammit!" I shouted and pulled the trigger. I felt the hammer slam into the firing pin.

"Stupid boy. I told you before that I am blessed. And here, at this altar, in this place of power, I am invincible."

I kept my stance between Harleaux and Bear and prayed for a new trick. He was barely conscious but still breathing. With breath, there was life, and with life, maybe some fleeting hope that I could figure a way out of this mess.

"So, that's what this is then? An altar? And I thought the bone catacombs in France were twisted."

The chickens bristled and shook their feathers. "Careful, Istenhegyi. The Loas do not take kindly to blasphemers."

I wiped the sweat off my forehead with the back of my hand. I kept flapping my lips, hoping some passing Muse would be kind to me. "So, this is what you do? Slice and dice men up for chickens? What kind of religion is that?"

"An effective one, Mr. Istenhegyi. Look at me." She did a little turn in her white gown. "Do you like what you see?" She moved towards me and leaned in so close I could smell the jasmine. "I am seventy-two years old. My children...I have twelve of them....prosper all across the country. They are businessmen, lawyers, teachers, doctors. They have succeeded in the world in spite of the color of their skin. All of this I owe to the power of the Loas."

"At a price." I nodded over at Bear. His breathing was getting ragged. "A hell of a steep one."

"You give tithes. You eat little crackers and sip on tiny cups of wine. This is just the same."

"I beg to differ."

"Hush!" she snapped. "My Love comes."

There was a rustling amongst the chickens as the flood of white split asunder to let the monster snake chicken come through. It walked slowly, picking up each thick taloned foot, and putting it down with exact pageantry. It held its head high like a monarch and swayed side to side. The chickens closest to it, bowed their heads as it walked past.

It walked up to Harleaux and rubbed its head across her belly and up between her breasts. I heard a deep cooing sound come from one of them. I can't promise it was from the bird.

"Step aside, Istenhegyi. It is time."

"Wait! Wait!" I said. "But you already tithed. The Isaac kid. Why do you need another?"

The monster snake chicken reared back its head as if it suddenly noticed me and hissed. Golden globs of spit rained down on me. They stung as they hit my skin. She shushed it and brushed down its feathers.

"I need two tributes this month. My son started up a new law firm in New York. To ensure his success, I needed Isaac. Then, my granddaughter went into labor. Those bastard doctors in Chicago butchered her." She stroked the monster snake chicken. "She would've died and left the baby motherless if my Love hadn't interceded.

"Now move aside. It is time for the tribute."

Two favors. Two tributes. My brain sizzled with an idea. But could I do it?

Do you really have a choice, kiddo?

I stood my ground. "Is it him you need? Him, specifically?"

"What do you mean?"

I looked at Bear. He was awake. A part of me hating him for that.

I put the muzzle up to his head.

He nodded and winked with his one good eye.

"Happy Birthday, Jake."

There was a horrible explosion and I felt my arm go numb.

Harleaux screamed. "What have you done?" She reached out for me with her manicured claws. I grabbed her and held her tight. "What have you done!?!?!"

The flock tightened around their King as its eyes began to glow a honey yellow gold. There was a low, hungry cawing generating from the floor. The Loa raised its head to full staff and waved it back and forth as golden slobber dripped off its beak.

"Time for the tribute, honey."

I pushed her towards the flock and she fell to her knees.

I ran and didn't look back when the screaming started.

CHAPTER TEN

Back in The Shed

The hellish noise outside is grating on my nerves.

My leg is bleeding from where one of them clawed me. The smell drives them crazy, beaks and spurs, punching through the slats, pounding against the pathetic excuse of a door in a frenzied pandemonium. The weakening door pushes me against the crate, breaking the jars inside. The smell of grain alcohol scorches my nostrils. *CHRIST! IT BURNS!* I grit my teeth against the fiery streaks of pain as the moonshine floods into the scratches and gouges in my back. Of course. Why not? I'm already covered in mud, shit and the blood of my best friend. What's a little moonshine?

"Go home and roost, damn you!" I yelled as I kicked at the door. The frame shuddered, threatened to splinter, just making them caw even louder.

It was useless. Not just my screaming at frenzied chickens that were determined as all hell to get at me, all of it was useless. My coming down here, play acting like a private eye, trying to save Bear...useless, completely stupidly useless.

I kicked the door again and listened to the ruckus crank up to another notch. It didn't help anything, I know, but kicking was more macho than crying.

It was so unfair. All Bear wanted was to live the lives of all those stupid heroes he read in his favorite pulp magazines. Impossible men tackling and winning against impossible odds. Tough guys in fedoras who always got the girl. Was that too much to ask?

I could feel the rage boiling deep inside my gut. Bear didn't deserve this. He was just doing his job. And to top it all, it was my birthday, damn it! By now, we should be roaring drunk, with beautiful girls in our laps and sitting down to a nice dinner of fried chicken and-

I smiled. Oh…. perhaps a bit too big for sanity's sake as the idea blossomed in my brain and I patted my pocket.   I felt the hard rectangle case. The smell of moonshine cinched my plan.

"You and me, Bear. We're burning this damn town down."

****

I opened the door of the shed. The horde of chickens went silent.

Maybe it was the fire was what held their attention. Or maybe it was the sight of me, shirtless, covered in blood and shit, with the toothy smile of a man who had been pushed one step too damn far.

I lobbed the first fireball straight into the throng, scattering them in all directions.

I stepped outside, holding high two more flaming bottles of moonshine.

"WHO IS READY FOR ANOTHER?!?!"

The dozen chickens tipped their heads to the side.

One of the cockier chickens took a step forward.

"WE HAVE A WINNER!" I said and smashed the bottle straight into it.

It cawed once and began running around, bashing into other chickens, and catching them alight. I tossed the second bottle at another one and it finished off the job for me. In no time, the whole damn dirty dozen were cooked ducks. Well, chickens. Whatever.

Now for phase two of Plan Big Chicken Dinner.

I dragged six of the cases over to the barn and set them strategically around the building. I opened a few more cases and splashed moonshine on the walls. The wood was dry and old. It wouldn't take much to bring this place down. I could hear thumping from inside. Chickens threw themselves against the door I had the foresight to close behind me after I ran out as Harleaux died. I threw the empty bottle against the door and heard their startled cries as it shattered. Ha! Stupid birds. Should've run while you could! Now you're trapped inside with your voodoo priestess bitch and your freak chicken snake god and…and…

Dammit, Bear.

My heart sank.

I flipped open my Zippo, pulled out my handkerchief and tossed the flaming cloth on the alcohol-soaked door.

"This is officially the worst birthday I have ever had."

****

I watched the fire consume the barn.

The walls fell first and then the ceiling followed. Everything inside would be crushed or burnt. By morning, there would be nothing left of the bodies but ashes and bones. No evidence to support my story. For the best, I suppose. I don't think the local police have a form for Death by Monster Chicken. Even in Louisiana.

I wished I had a cigarette. I don't smoke; it just seemed appropriate. The bloodied hero after defeating his archenemy, lighting up a cigarette as he walked away, alone, into the sunset. It's exactly the way the pulp stories always ended. I think Bear would have liked that.

While considering my options of finding a cab that would take back to town a half-naked man, bloodied and covered in shit, a horrible croaking scream came ripping from the sky. I looked up to see Harleaux's monster snake chicken king shoot up from the blazing barn. It crashed down to earth a few feet away from me.

It cawed deeply and pulled itself up off the ground. It had tripled in size and now stood a foot taller than me as if my blasphemy made it blossom. It cocked its head to the side, stared at me with hate filled golden eyes and scratched the ground with thick, calloused talons.

"KER-CAWWWWWW!" it bellowed. Yellow pus dripped from its fang-filled beak. Fangs? When did it grow teeth? Christ. The venom dripping from its mouth pooled on the ground and sizzled, turning the ground into a black ichor.

"Good chicken." I said as I reached behind me for the .38 I had stashed in my belt. Bear always warned me against doing that. "More dumbasses lose their balls that way." he said but when you shred your shirt into strips to make firebombs, some safety procedures are sacrificed.

I took a step backwards. "Nice chicken."

It snarled.

Wait. Did a chicken just snarl at me? Can chickens do that without lips?

It's amazing where my mind goes when faced with certain, grisly death.

Focus, Jake!

A wall in the altar room fell inwards. The chicken thing stumbled and then shook its head, spraying the acid. A drop landed on my shoulder. I could feel my skin bubble. I wiped it off with my hand. I gritted my teeth against the pain and used both hands to aim my gun. I had one bullet left. Would this even work? I remembered what happened with Harleaux. How effective would a gun be against a god?

It ker-cawed deeply and lowered its head like a bull getting readying to charge.

The chicken loa reared back its head and stared down at me. It slowly lifted a leg, pulling up its thick talons, readying to kick. A kick that would surely knock my head off my shoulders if it made contact.

A wall of the barn slumped in and the bird staggered.

Oh-ho! Pieces of the puzzle began to fall into place.

"Your place of power. Is that it? As it falls, you fall?" I could hear the fire eating away the walls. Soon, nothing would remain of the place. "Is that all you got...*chicken*?"

It shook its head, splattering more of the golden acid on the ground, reared back, screamed, "KER-CAWWWW!" and charged.

I aimed straight for its chest. The bullet ripped through its chest, exploding its heart.

It plopped over in the dirt, dead.

I stood there trying to think up something witty. All those pulp heroes had something clever to say as they stood over their archenemies. It was the calling card of the superhero. But I wasn't a hero. I was just a guy who had the great fortune of renting a space to Barrington Gunn, private investigator, who let me tag along on adventures and make- pretend I was his Watson.

But...what would that guy say?

I thought for half a second. A grin slid over my face.

"Why did the chicken cross the road?" I kicked dirt in the monster's face and sneered, "To get its ass kicked. That's why."

I bet that would've been better with a cigarette.

The End

JAKE ISTENHEGYI:

THE ACCIDENTAL DETECTIVE

Book Two

Golems, Goons

and

Cold Stone Bitches

This story is dedicated to Gunny Kohl, the inspiration for Bear Gunn. He would often tell me, "Nik, I don't care what you believe in but, goddammit, you gotta believe in something!"

R.I.P. John Kohl

The Utility Room

I stumble and barely make it inside the 'utility room' just before they can get to me.

I throw myself against the heavy security door, slamming it shut and then slide down to the floor. The only thing keeping my guts from falling out is my fist plugging up the hole where my stomach used to be. Blood is seeping through my fingers, keeping my hand warm while the rest of me gets colder.

In my other hand is a miracle that the people on the other side of the door are willing to kill me to get.

The hinges on the door start to scream as it slowly opens. I push against it, trying to close the damn thing but my feet slide in the blood that has pooled underneath me. I can't get any traction. Dammit! The door opens a fraction more…and a hand clutching a bloody knife shoves its way in.

My name is Jake Istenhegyi and this is how it ends. With me slip sliding in a pool of my own blood, trying to keep my guts from spilling out on the floor with a beautiful, psychotic maniac knocking down my door.

It's been one hell of a week.

Two Guys, Doing Their Job

A fire burning this far into the bayou wasn't going to be getting any attention any time soon so I sat cross legged on the ground and watched the flames for no other reason than to make sure that it was over. No surprises, no twist ending. Harleaux was dead and her monster chickens had died with her.

The smell of grilled chicken made my stomach growl.

My brain recoiled in disgust.

Mea culpa. The stomach wants what the stomach wants.

I also wanted to pay tribute to my friend, Bear Gunn, whose ashes would be mingled in forever with the bitch that killed him.

On top of that, I was too bone dead tired to move.

The rest of that night is a blur; I don't know how I made it out of the bayou. I found myself on a road and I hitchhiked home. Thank God for Southern hospitality. The sun had cracked over the horizon when I finally got back to the Odyssey Shop.

The Odyssey Shop was on the ground floor of the three-story building that I called home. There is a sign over the door: *We Go to the Ends of the Earth to Satisfy Your Needs!* I always thought that was a bit boastful considering that we stock books that were filled with more silverfish than paper and bric-a-brac too ordinary to list. The building is a beautiful piece of architecture, for those into that sort of thing. It was built in 1880's, red brick with wrought iron balconies on the third and second floor. I inherited it five years ago when my Uncle Andor stepped in front of a delivery truck. It was a hell of a way for a world traveler, drunk and scholar to exit but no one was really surprised. My father and his brothers never spoke of Andor unless the words 'bastard' and 'scandal' were involved. He was the grayish-black sheep of the Istenhegyi clan, sent off to New Orleans from Budapest to avoid smudging up the family name in yet another scrap with the law. The irony of being sent here in his stead is not lost on me. The Istenhegyi family has never minced words when it came to me, their inconvenient Romany half-breed progeny. Dear Uncle Andor wasn't the only brother who dallied with scandal and got caught. I'm the constant and irritating proof of that. Oh, sure, dear old Dad tells people he sent me away to save me from the clutches of the Nationalist Socialist Party. For that, I'm thankful but what he never mentions is the addendum that if I wanted to keep my trust fund flush, I had to step into Uncle Andor's shoes, no matter how much they stank.

And standing here, covered in blood and chicken shit, I could write a book on stink. I needed a shower and fast.

I started to put my key in the door when I noticed it was slightly ajar. And there were scuff marks around the doorjamb. I heard noises coming from the garden patio.

Oh, hell, what now?

The noises turned into voices. Gruff, angry, male voices.

"Dammit! Hold up your end!"

"You hold up your end! This sonofabitch is heavy! And hold up that damn flashlight. Can't see a goddamn thing!"

I pulled out the empty pistol from my belt and went to investigate. Because that's the best plan of action for a person on the brink of exhaustion and covered in blood and chicken shit.

I scooted against the wall to the corner and peeked. There were two men in the garden. Two very large, black men wrestling a crate out of the 'utility room'.

That room is a mystery to me. Mama Effie has never let me go near it. I own the building, true, but she runs it.

And I don't think she'd take it well if I just stood here and let these goons steal from her.

Did I mention these guys were huge? And my gun was empty?

I stepped out from behind an elephant ear, holding the gun out in front of me. "Hey!" I shouted, my voice not squeaky at all. "Drop that!"

The two men looked up at me and then at each other.

"Listen to this guy," said one of them, grinning.

And they ignored me and continued carrying the crate into the utility room.

"Now, I'm serious! I own this building! Look, I've got a gun! Stop before I-"

Wait. Are they going INTO the utility room?

Confused, I dropped my gun to my side. "What the hell are you guys doing?"

"Our goddamn jobs, rube," said a man behind me. Right before he bashed me on the head and made everything go dark.

Trouble Comes in Threes

When I opened my eyes, there was a grinning satyr leaning over me, offering me grapes.

I was on a raised stage. There were empty sockets for lights all around the edge and the gilded satyrs were poised on either side. On a mural behind me, a Bacchanalian orgy raged of pink and brown women of generous proportions being serviced and fondled by thick, muscle bound men and tongue wagging satyrs in a Grecian pool. All in all, everyone seemed to be getting as good as they got.

Off stage, where the audience would sit, there were crates, dozens of them, of all shapes and sizes. Hanging from the ceiling, there were three large crystal chandeliers. Only one of them, the middle one, was lit with electric lights.

I was alone.

I scooted to the edge of the stage. Every movement seemed to jar something loose in the back of my head. I hopped down and walked over to a crate. It was as high as my thigh and heavy as lead. The lid was nailed shut. I looked around and found a crowbar leaning up against the stage. I popped the lid and a cloud of dust and mold flew into my face. I waved away the soot, coughing and gagging. Once it had settled, I looked inside to see a stack of what looked like dusty rags. Looking closer, I could see skeletal fingers tearing through the rags. It was a box of mummies, stacked six deep.

A door opened and the three men from the patio came inside.

Mama Effie walked in behind them.

"Well, well, boys. Look who has joined the party." she said.

She pushed a button on the wall and the other two chandeliers came to life. The entirety of the room was open to me and I could see an intricately carved oak bar with a gaudy, gold framed mirror on the wall. There were dusty and broken scattered barstools around. The floor was a ruined parquetry of chipped black and white tiles. On the walls were more murals of beautiful men and women doing what beautiful men and women do.

"Why are there mummies in my utility room? And what the hell is with the stage? And all the lights? What kind of utility room is this?"

"Welcome to the Odyssey Shop, Mr. Istenhegyi. Well, the proper one, anyway. I had been waiting for the right time to tell you but….eh." She shrugged her shoulders. "Things were going so well, I figured, why bother?"

"What the hell are you doing with mummies? What is in the rest of these crates?"

"Booze, pornography, a few odds and ends. You ever wonder why it is called the Odyssey Shop? Why the sign out front says *We Go To The Ends of the Earth to Satisfy your Needs?*"

I shrugged.

"Anything you wanted; you could find it here." She winked. "Anything."

The murals surrounding me took on a deeper meaning. This wasn't art; it was a goddamn menu.

"Christ. Am I living in a goddamn whorehouse?"

Mama Effie slapped me hard enough to make my ears ring, compounding the already nauseating headache. Her three goons gathered up behind her.

"You will watch your language in front of me, *boy*. I won't stand for it. I am a Lady. My family has been working this city for five generations. A hundred years before your Dalmatian immigrant ass crawled its way out of the Danube and found its way here!"

Dalmatian. I'll never understand that slur. It's what the locals called anyone of Eastern European blood. In some quarters, we're looked down on more than the Gypsies back home. But seriously….Dalmatian? What does that even mean?

I put my hands up in submission. That seemed to appease her, and Mama Effie's eyes softened. Her goons eased up as well.

"You should have seen her back in her glory days, boy. Only the best of New Orleans society was allowed through those doors. All the big names played here. So many beautiful people came here to dance, to drink and to play. Back in the day, this was the place to be seen if you were anyone of any breeding." Mama Effie took a deep breath. "It's a shame, what she's become."

"My uncle ran a speakeasy? What happened? Why all the crates?"

"When Prohibition ended …" She waved her long red fingernails in the air. "Well, things happened. It's a long story. The Odyssey Shop's glory days were done. Now she is just a shell, a storage place. Haven't you ever wondered why trucks would make deliveries but none of the stock ever changed?"

I stared at her, not wanting to say anything that would make me sound any stupider than I already felt. "I didn't pay attention…I thought you took care of all that."

"That's why I like you. Such a stupid boy." She patted my cheek. "And because I take care of everything, you and your little detective friend get to play Cowboys and Indians all the live long day."

A heavy ball was sinking in my gut. "Jesus. So, let me see if I understand this. Uncle Andor ran a shell business for who? The mob?"

Then a more immediate realization washed over me like a cold shower.

"Wait, am I running a shell business for the mob? Did my father send me out here to keep peace with…oh, nononono….I didn't sign up for this! No, I'm done. I'm out. After everything else I have been through tonight, I am out!"

"I'm sorry you feel that way," said Mama Effie. "Your Uncle had a similar bout of conscience. Turned out to be fatal. Boys, see to Mr. Istenhegyi."

"What- ooof!"

The first punch in my gut bent me in half. The second one in my kidneys put me down on the floor. I stayed there, gasping for breath, doing my best not to vomit.

Mama Effie kneeled, grabbed a fistful of my hair and pulled my head off the floor. "Stupid boy," she hissed in my face. "You didn't just inherit Mr. Andor's building, you inherited his debt as well. And there are certain persons that expect to see it paid. With interest. Do you understand? Andor wasn't just our business face but a customer. And he had very peculiar, expensive tastes. Then he tried to leave without paying his bills. Well...you don't think he willingly walked in front of that bus, do you?"

Someone kicked me in the kidney to make sure I understood.

Message received.

She let go of my hair and my head bounced on the floor. "Now, tomorrow we go back to business as usual. Pretending to the world at large that you're the boss and I'm the loyal employee."

I grunted something that she took as acceptance. Frankly, I didn't have it in me to do much more.

She patted my cheek. "My sweet idiot. Pick up him, boys. We're finished here."

The boys dragged me back in the store, dropped me on the floor next to the counter and left through the front door.

"I'll be back to open the store in a few hours." Mama Effie said. "I suggest you get cleaned up. You're a disgraceful mess."

I heard the click of the door locking behind her. Locking out any hope I had for getting out of New Orleans.

I grabbed the counter and pulled myself up. I stood there for what felt like a thousand years, trying to get my throbbing, bleeding head around everything that had happened in just twelve hours.

My apartment was on the third floor. I climbed that flight of stairs like I was climbing Mt. Everest. My heart, body and mind either hurt, screamed, or felt like lead. I just wanted to shower the last twenty-four hours off my body and pray that I didn't piss blood before climbing into bed.

Little did I know what was waiting upstairs for me.

She was laying outside Bear's office. A petite thing, platinum blonde hair cut in a long bob that fell like a curtain over her face. She was barefoot, wearing a blue raincoat that she gripped tightly around her

I remembered the front door and how it had been jimmied. Was this our burglar? Or maybe just a drunk looking for a place to crash. Or perhaps a client looking for Bear?

Then I noticed the blood pooling beside her.

"Miss?" I tapped her on the shoulder. "Miss? Are you all right? Can I get you some help?"

She gasped as if she were fighting for air and looked up at me. Her big, gray eyes were filled with pain and fear. She was so pale that I could make out a highway of blue veins beneath her skin. She stood up, wobbling like a newborn calf. "Barrington Gunn?" she said, her voice trembling as she held out a folded piece of stationary. I took it and stuffed it in my pants pocket.

"No, my name is Jake-"

Her eyes rolled back, and she fell towards me. I caught her, nearly falling under her dead weight, and laid her down. Her coat opened and exposed her nude and very bloody body. I counted five stab wounds in her midriff. I bent over her, feeling for a pulse. It was weak and fading.

Just then, the mystery lady grabbed my shirt and pulled me down. For a woman bleeding to death on my floor, she was horribly strong. She pulled me closer to her porcelain face and brushed her lips against my ear.

"Mr. Gunn, tell me…has it come? Do you have it?" Her voice was soft, but I could hear a slight Italian accent, very faint. "Is it here? Am I too late?"

"I'm sorry but I don't know what you mean."

Her eyes snapped open and flashed a terrible sadness that made a knife turn in my chest. "Oh, dear…" she gasped. "Am I too early?"

The mystery lady groaned and arched her back in a painful convulsion, yanking me with her with every spasm. I grabbed her by her shoulders and held her so she wouldn't hurt herself. She coughed and spurted out a bloody spray that splattered in my face.

"ISTENEM!" *GOD!* I shouted, wildly wiping the blood off my face.

Her hands clawed at me as she shook twice more and then went completely still.

I laid her down, trying to avoid getting more blood on me. I looked at her face. Her fading, gray eyes were staring at me, cold and so very dead.

They say that trouble always travels in threes. It goes to figure that the dead mystery lady laying at my feet finished off the night.

Chapter Four

A Few Hours Rest

I was still seeing white spots from the crime photographer's flash when the morgue boys came to take my mystery lady away. I can't imagine the camera did her much justice. She really was quite a looker underneath all that blood.

Mama Effie wasn't happy to come back to a shop full of cops. Once she settled into her throne behind the register, she relaxed. She and a few of the older officers shared stories of the old days and I saw a few hidden winks here and there.

The homicide detective, Detective Reggie Collins came soon after. He was around fifty years old, had a very sallow complexion and stunk of old cigarettes and had coffee breath. He slouched around the hallway uncomfortably in his beige suit and tugged at his tie as if it were a noose.

"So, Mr. Ist…Isten-"

"Ishten-hedgy." I dramatically over-pronounced my surname. It's a common problem.

"Ishtenhedgy." He imitated me. "Let me see if I have this straight. So, this lady breaks into your building, you find her here, sitting on the stairs."

"Yes."

"She rushes you, collapses at your feet, and then dies."

I nodded.

"You have that effect on a lot of women?"

"Luckily, no."

"Uh-huh. So, and you said you think she was here to hire a private detective?"

"She thought I was Bear. It is a sound deduction."

"Uh-huh. Do you know where Bear is now?"

The image of a burning barn flashed into my head.

"Nem." I slipped into Hungarian when I got stressed. "I mean, no. I do not."

"Humph. Damn. The bastard owes me five dollars."

"Do you want me to come to the precinct to file a report?" I asked, trying to be helpful. I was pooling all the pulp legalese I had gleaned from reading Bear's magazine collection. In those stories, the coppers always pulled people down to the precinct for statements, whatever that meant

He pulled a toothpick out of his lapel pocket and chewed on it, smiling. "Naw. No need for more paperwork for a Jane Doe." He shook his notepad. "I got all I need here from you and Mama Effie. We'll float her picture around. If we're lucky, maybe somebody will come for her. I can't promise anything. It's been a hot summer. If she goes unclaimed, they won't keep her long. She'll end up in Potter's Field. Damn shame. I bet she was a pretty thing, under all that blood."

After the police left, Mikey ran up the stairs with baking soda and a mop. Within minutes, the floor was as if she had never existed. My father, the philosopher academic, would have said there was a lesson to be learned here.

God, I needed a drink. But, first, a shower.

I scraped off my clothes and took a long, hot shower. Soap stung my eyes as I covered myself in lemon scented lather. I scrubbed my washcloth into strips trying to get the scum from the last few days out of my skin. It didn't matter; I still felt dirty. I pressed my forehead against the wall and relished the pain as the scourging hot water beat down the back of my neck. I saw the water, streaked with blood and God only knows what else, circle down the drain.

I really, really needed a drink.

My flat was a maze of boxes and crates left behind by Uncle Andor. Five years had gone by and I still felt like a squatter.

The apartment's layout was simple. It had a front room that could be used as a parlor or an office bisected by pocket doors from a living space with a small kitchen and bathroom in the back. That is where I had made my camp amongst all the left behind souvenirs of Uncle Andor's life. I had a bed, a dresser, some books and my one prized possession: a painting. It was done by a woman I knew for a summer in Paris. Andrea. She was a dabbler. Paints, sculpture, men. She had her hand in most everything. The painting itself isn't particularly good from an artistic standpoint. It's an amateurish Impressionist piece, done with more passion than precision. A woman is dressing or undressing, depending on your point of view, and a dark-haired man waits in the bed behind her. I remember the night that inspired it vividly. Andrea gave the painting to me as a gift before she went back home to Italy…and her fiancé. Like I said, she was a dabbler. The same, I guess, could be said for me.

I fell into my unkempt bed naked and soaking wet from the shower. I wasn't doing my sheets any favors and

God only knew what kind of rat's nest my hair would be in the morning but, to hell with it; I'd deal with the consequences when I woke up. If I woke up. Frankly, I didn't care which happened if I could have a few hours not hurting or caring about anything. Just a few hours. The world would keep turning while I turned my head off for just a few hours…

****

I woke up with two things pounding in unison. One was my head and the other was the door.

"What?!" I yelled at the closed door.

The pounding stopped and a young boy's voice answered. "Mama Effie told me to tell you …" The rest was muffled behind the door.

I was in no mood for any of Mama Effie's shenanigans. I wrapped my bed sheet around me, stumbled to the door and tore it open. "Spit it out, kid!" Mikey looked up at me with eyes crazy with fear. "What?!"

"You have a client!" The boy said before he ran away as if I were going to chase him with a hickory stick.

"Mr. Barrington Gunn?"

You know that feeling when you are standing in front of something impossibly, classically beautiful, like a Grecian statue come to life, while you are wearing nothing but a bed sheet damp from last night's shower? If you don't, be grateful. I don't have the vocabulary in English to describe how much of a *vesztes* I felt like at that very moment.

Her hair was honey blonde and fell in waves around her shoulders. Her eyes were slate gray, set deep in her alabaster skin. She painted her lips a deep plum. God, I wanted to bite them. She was wearing loose, wide legged cuffed cream-colored silk trousers and a matching low-cut blouse, classically chic for a summer in New Orleans. Although, I doubt she could sweat. Nothing that perfect would do something so human.

"Mr. Gunn?" she said again.

"Um, no." I tried to finger comb my hair into some respectful sort of rat's nest and nearly dropped my bed sheet. "Sorry. Mr. Gunn is unavailable. Out of town. Don't know when he'll be back. I'm Jake Istenhegyi, his associate. Please forgive my appearance. If you'll give me a few minutes to get dressed..."

"I'm sorry but I don't really have the time to spare. Can I come in?"

A beautiful woman asks to come into my home while I am basically naked? What else do I say?

"Yes, please."

She entered and I could smell cinnamon as she walked by.

I gathered up my toga and moved some boxes off a leather couch, dusting it off with the edge of my sheet. "Excuse the mess."

"Are you moving?" she said as she sat down.

"No, just really never settled in."

"Are you...well? You look like you had a rough night."

"Ah, well. Yes." I touched the goose egg on my forehead gingerly. "One of the pitfalls of the trade. Can I get you something to drink? Water? I could put a kettle on for tea or coffee?"

She shook her head. I did a silent prayer of thanks since I didn't have tea or coffee and, frankly, I wouldn't drink what comes out of that faucet on a bet.

I perched myself on the couch next to her, making sure all my delicates were still properly covered. "How can I help you?"

"My name is Piera Lombardi. Mr. Gunn has a package for me. I was hoping to collect it. Today, if possible." She retrieved a letter from her purse and gave it to me carefully folded it so only one paragraph was revealed.   It was on heavy stationery, expensive, with lavender infused into the paper. It was written in Italian.

"Do you need me to translate it for you?"

"No. One of the many fringe benefits of a childhood being bounced around every boarding school in Europe is picking up a handful of languages."

The letter, from what she let me see, read:

I have entrusted the Seed to an honorable man. Other than my Archibald, he is the most trustworthy soul I have ever known. His name is Barrington Gunn, 3574 Magazine Street, New Orleans, Louisiana. Go to him when the time is right. Whoever receives it first must take care of it. That is all I ask. Please grant this favor to a terribly old, dying woman.

She took it away before I could unfold it and see any more of the letter.

"What is the Seed?" I asked.

"A family heirloom." She waved the question away with glossy polished nails. "My sister, Giovanna, loved games. This is her attempt at one last scavenger hunt."

"She's dead then?"

Piera shrugged. "I would think so. We weren't close. She was ten years my senior and, as the years rolled on, the gap grew even wider. But that's not important." She smiled and dazzled any questions I had out of my head. "Can I see if Mr. Gunn has my package?"

"Yes…yes. Just let me get dressed. I'll take you up to his office, it's downstairs. Just one second…"

"Fine. Please hurry. I am on a schedule."

I gathered my sheet together, went through the pocket doors and closed them.

"Clothes, clothes, clothes." I muttered like an idiot as I ransacked through my dresser. I pulled out a clean undershirt, underwear, socks. I put them on while hop skipping as awkwardly as my bruised ribs allowed towards the closet for some pants and an unwrinkled dress shirt. I nearly fell on my face when my foot got snagged on the pair of dirty pants from the night before. Christ! I kicked them aside and the letter the dead girl gave me fell out of my pocket. The stationery was the same and I instantly smelled the lavender infusion. I picked it up.

It read:

My dearest sisters,

The time has come again. I hope this letter finds you in good repair. As the years roll by, it becomes harder to keep things together, does it not? Especially you, dear Pia, such a life you lead…but I promised myself I would not preach to you. Not this time.

I am giving the Salt to you as I have decided to end this charade. Without my Archibald and my sweet boy, Arthur, by my side, life is too hard, this body too confining. I long to be with them more than I desire to continue living on this Earth.

I have entrusted the Seed to an honorable man. Other than my Archibald, he is the most trustworthy soul I have ever known. His name is Barrington Gunn, 3574 Magazine Street, New Orleans, Louisiana. Go to him when the time is right. Please take care of it. That is all I ask. Please grant this favor to a terribly old dying woman.

God speed you on your journey, Sisters. I know there is bad blood between you two and, if I were a better sibling, I would build a bridge between you two but I simply do not have the energy. Please, in memory of our father who loved us in his own misguided way, be kind to one another.

Please pray for me, if you still do such trivialities, that I find my Archibald and Arthur in Heaven.

Eternally yours,

Giovanna Lucia Lombardi-Bonham

I stared at the letter and mentally compared the flowing penmanship. This was a duplicate of the one Piera showed me. "Curiouser and curiouser."

A tapping at the door broke the spell. "Mr. Istenhegyi? Are you ready? Please, I don't have much time to spare."

"One minute!" I finish dressing and slipped the letter inside my pocket.

She was waiting for me at the door. "Well, you clean up nicely."

"Thanks." Oddly, now her glamour was lost on me. Her hair looked too brassy and her lips looked bruised and flat. Being played does that to a guy like me. "Let me grab my keys and I'll take you to his office."

Chapter Five

Keeping Up Appearances

We didn't find anything. It wasn't any surprise to me but my mysterious visitor, Piera Lombardi, was not amused. She did a good job hiding her anger but, by the way the veins in her neck throbbed as her jaw clenched, I could see cracks in the veneer.

"I don't think mail has run today. Perhaps we will get lucky and it will come in the next few hours," I said.

It was a lie. He didn't trust anything to come to the office. Bear had a special deal with guys at the post office to route everything to his post office box. I used to think that was an affectation but now I wonder how much he knew about the Odyssey Shop's true business.

"Give me your contact information and I'll get back in touch when it comes."

"Fine." She ripped off a piece off the desk blotter and scribbled a hotel name and a phone number. "Please. Call me as soon as possible."

And she left without even a backward glance.

The bruises from last night were darkening and my back was feeling tighter. *Good.* Pain is always a good motivator. I listened for the tinkle of the bell as she went out the door and waited ten minutes.

From the stairs, I could see the layout of the shop below.

Mama Effie was sitting in her throne at the register, holding court with three men. Two were older gentleman, Creole, like herself, wearing linen suits. The third was a young, white man in stained trousers and a white undershirt. She handed each a thick envelope. She nodded at them and they left without a word.

The two goons from last night were settled around the round bistro table in the corner, sitting comfortably in overstuffed chairs having a coffee and reading the paper. One of them was only barely moving his lips. Color me impressed.

I went downstairs, whistling. If they wanted me to play Boss, then I needed to put on a show.

"Hello, boys." I said as I snatched the paper out of Goon #1's hands. "Need to check the news, thanks!" I ruffled through it as I walked over to the register. There was nothing about the fire in the bayou. That was good. It was only a matter of time but the longer it remained unnoticed, the more evidence of what happened would be destroyed.

The Dead Girl made the paper. Page three, above the fold. Terrible photo. Some people don't look good in black and white. There was a quick paragraph under the picture, asking for any information, blah, blah. I tore the page out for the picture more than for the article.

"Hey!" Goon #1 stood up, nearly toppling over the table. "I bought that paper!"

"Take it out of the register." I folded the rest of the paper and tossed it to him. "I'm keeping this bit for my files."

"Well, well, well." Mama Effie tapped her fingers on the counter. "Somebody seems to be full of beans this afternoon."

"Just keeping up appearances. Me boss, you employees. I'll be out for the rest of the afternoon, on business. Take any messages for me."

"Certainly, *boss.*" Her lips curled into a smile. "And what about Bear Gunn?"

My bravado wobbled. "Wh-what about him?"

Her smile grew a touch wider, like a snake unhinging its jaw. "Just wanted to know what to say should people ask. Where is he? When is he returning? You know, the usual sort of questions people ask."

What did she know? How could she know anything? Her eyes were unreadable. Two dark pits that I felt on the verge of falling into forever. "Tell them that he is on sabbatical for the foreseeable future."

"Oh? On a sabbatical?" She laughed and clapped her hands. "Did you hear that, boys? Bear Gunn is on a sabbatical. Oh, that is rich."

"Yeah." Goon #1 snapped his paper open.

Goon #2 just nodded and coughed out a laugh.

My bravado slipped and fell around my feet like dirty trousers.

"Well, don't let us hold you back. Go on, attend to your business, *boss*."

Chapter Six

The Pick Up

I could still hear her laughing as the door slammed shut behind me.

Damn!

See what she does? She gets right under a man's skin and then burrows, laying down her seeds of doubt that squirm and itch. What does she know about Bear? How can she know anything?

Hell, the damn woman probably didn't know anything but now, because of the way I reacted like a pup caught pissing on a rug, she knows something is definitely worth finding out about. And that is all the bait a bitch in her sort of business needs.

She'll use it against me, lock down her grip on my balls even tighter.

Damn it all to hell!

It's a forty-five-minute walk to the post office on St. Charles. Normally, I'd get a cab, especially in this heat but, damn it, I needed to feel my feet stomp on the sidewalk, something to release the churning steam inside my gut.

After a block or two of grumbling and kicking stones, I calmed down and started to think. What was I planning on doing if the package was in Bear's post office box? Give it to Piera? Why should I? Who was she? Was the dead girl her sister? What the hell was going on with my mystery woman, the dead girl and the missing package? What the hell is in it? Who is Giovanna Bonham anyway? An old client? Someone who kept him on retainer? She was definitely someone before my time with him. I made a mental note to check through Bear's old files when I returned home.

The post office Bear frequented was an annex on St. Charles Street. The postmaster, Klaus, was a big, fat fellow, with white hair and a full white beard and he ran it like a benevolent tyrant. He would trash what he thought were naughty packages, like certain magazines that were mailed in brown paper, and hand deliver packages he deemed good, like cookies, often expecting a small stipend for the service, i.e. a cookie. Sure, it was crooked as hell but everybody loved Klaus.

"Hi-ho, Jake!" he bellowed. Everything he did was big. I suppose a man that size couldn't help but fill the space around him.

"Good afternoon, Klaus." I said as I passed by the clerk's desk.

There was a wall of post boxes, about fifty or so. Each box had a bronze gilded front with a face that read 1-0 and a brass arrow dial. I found Bear's box, dialed the combination, and opened the door. Inside were some envelopes and a green slip of paper that informed me of a package waiting at the desk.

Bingo.

I gave the slip to Klaus. He read it and looked over his half-moon spectacles at me. "Well, now, you aren't Barrington Gunn."

"He is gone. Out of town. He asked me to look after his mail. While…while he was…gone…sir."

"Well, I guess since it's you, Jake, I can trust you. You tell Bear that I said hello, will you? He's one of my favorite people!"

I swallowed hard. Lying to Santa Claus, even a fake one, had to be a mortal sin. "Yes, sir."

"Oh ho! Let's go look and see what you've got!" And Klaus hoisted his generous belly out of his seat and went to check the elves…I mean, the shelves.

While he was gone, I suddenly had a prickly sensation that made the hairs on my neck stand up, as if someone was watching me. I reached back to rub the three crescent shaped scars on the back of my neck. I've had the scars for as long as I can remember although I don't quite know where they came from. I just know that when they appeared, my mother disappeared. My father would never speak of them. Or of her.

They prickled when something was wrong. Like the winter when I was a kid and was outside sledding, I had a weird prickle and was able to duck out of the way of a runaway sled. It was weird but kept me out of a lot of scrapes. The family cook teased and called them my Witch's Mark. I thought it was funny, but my father didn't see the humor; he fired her shortly afterwards.

I looked around the small office. Nothing seemed out of whack. I went to the door and looked outside. Very few people were outside suffering the afternoon heat. A slump shouldered mother trying to herd her three kids on the sidewalk, a few young black guys throwing dimes against a wall and a man in a suit window shopping. Nothing seemed out of place, but my neck kept right on prickling.

Klaus came back with one box. A small thing, about the size of a paperback novel, wrapped in brown paper and twine. "Here you go! Must be more of those detective story books Bear loves."

I nodded my head as I scooped the box up. The postmark was from Giovanna Bonham in Boston. "Thanks, Klaus. I'll make sure he gets it."

"You be good, Jake!" Klaus said and waved goodbye. "And promise to tell Bear I said hello!"

"Will do, sir!" I said, smiling and waving. I was definitely going to hell.

Leaving the post office, I stepped out into a wall of oppressive heat. Probably just a taste of what I'm can expect is waiting for me if I continue lying to Santa. I started down St. Charles, tossing the package up and down, a one-handed juggling act to pass the time, and looked for a cab to take me home.

The back of my neck was prickling like crazy. I rolled my shoulders trying to ease the itchiness. Damn, it was annoying. I stashed the package in my back pocket and looked around. There was still nothing…wait, except the man I saw window shopping, the well-dressed man in the suit, he was a block behind me but gaining fast.

I took another look and now there were two of them. Side by side, walking in unison, like windup soldiers. Handsome guys if matinee idols were your thing. Chiseled jaw, straight nose, deep set eyes and wavy blonde hair with enough pomade fingered into it to drown a duck.

Soon, a third man of the same cut joined them, completing the line and taking up the rear.

The prickling was turning into a drilling pain. I took a quick look over my shoulder, smiled and nodded.

They picked up their pace.

Shit! I jackrabbited straight down St. Charles, cutting into an alleyway, flipping over a full trashcan as I passed. I didn't stop to look behind me but from the constant rat-a-tat-tat of their shoe leather slapping the pavement, I don't think it slowed them down much.

The alley leads out to Grover Street where a dozen restaurants and food stalls did business. There were people meandering up and down the sidewalks. I could barely get through them without knocking some poor git into the gutter. So, restaurants meant trash and that meant more alley ways. I looked for the closest one and ducked down it, took a left past some bins down another alleyway and then took a right straight into a brick wall.

"Shit!"

The trio turned the corner and trapped me inside the trash strewn cul-de-sac. The three of them advanced at me completely in unison. Right, left, right left, face first, hands to their side. I half expected one of them to start doing the can-can.

"Come on, gentlemen" I held my hands, palms up. "There is no reason for violence, is there? Look at your nice suits. You don't want to get them all mucked up with my blood? I sure don't want you to. Let's settle this over a cold beer- Hey!"

The men on the far left and right stepped forward, grabbed my arms and forced me back to the wall. They held my hands high above my head; my feet left the ground.

The man in the middle walked up to me and started rummaging through my shirt.

"Hey, hey!" I twisted as best I could. "Can't you buy a guy a drink first?"

He started towards my pants, putting his hands down my pockets, searching, and finding more than I wanted him to find.

"Whoa-ho-ho! Back off, now! That's enough, buddy-boy! I don't know what sort of man you take me for!" I pulled my legs up and mule kicked the son of a bitch straight into the wall behind him.

He slammed into the wall, his head jerking back like a puppet on a string. He stood there, frozen and I wondered if he wasn't impaled on something jutting out from the building.

His buddies were still holding me tight. "You guys wanna go check on him?"

They were a still and silent as Grabby McFingers. A strange black was growing out from his temples, cracking out like spidery fingers over his forehead. They finally met in the middle and then began splitting downwards on Grabby's face. There was no blood, not a drop. It was like watching a boulder be struck with a very precise hammer as his face split in two. Yellow and orange sand began seeping from the cracks, running down his face like tears. A wisp of smoke began to funnel up from the top of his head and red lava shot up in one single blast, burning the brick wall behind in black. Grabby McFingers slid down the wall and fell over in a heap.

I struggled and twisted, trying to get free from the absolutely rock-hard grips of Dumble Dee and Dumble Dumbnuts. All I succeeded in doing was rubbing my wrists raw. Worse than that, I could feel my pants slowly slipping down. I tried to rub my backside up against the wall in a vain attempt to pull my trousers up.

I felt something snag. The package I had put in my back pocket fell to the ground and skittered into the alleyway.

D.D. and Dumbnuts suddenly let me go and I fell on my ass.

They both went for the box.

"So, that's the game, then?" I crawled on all fours, right through their legs, grabbed the package, go to my feet and ran like the devil was chasing me.

I made it to St. Charles again, out of breath and desperate for a cab. There wasn't one anywhere! Dammit! I could hear their running footsteps coming up through the alleyway behind me. There had to be a cab somewhere! I took a step off the curb to see if I could flag something down and a silver Packard swerved, damn near running me down, and did a dead stop in front of me.

"What the hell!" I screamed at the driver. "Are you trying to kill me?"

She turned and smiled. Her face was still pale but there was life in her eyes that wasn't there the last time I saw her. "No, you delicious idiot, I'm trying to save you. Get in before they get here!"

And that's how I hitched a ride home with a dead girl.

Chapter Seven

A Ride with a Dead Girl

A half dozen or more empty bottles rattled around my feet as I climbed into the Packard. I barely closed the door when she slammed the gas pedal to the floor, slamming me against the seat.

"Hold on to your family jewels, pretty boy!" she cackled as she tore down the street. "It's going to get a little crazy in here!'

She barreled down St. Charles, took a right onto Milan and then nearly set the car on two wheels taking a left onto Perrier Street.

I tried talking to her, hoping it would get her to slow down. "What were those things back there? One guy's head split right in two!"

"Oh, you broke one? Ooooh, Piera is going to be mad at you, pretty boy. She makes them from scratch, you know. Old family recipe. I'm Pia, by the way, the baby sister. Oh look, a fruit stand! Watch this!"

She sped up, expertly clipped the vendor's table leg so that the whole thing splintered, spilling apples, pears and God knows what else into the street.

"Jesus! Slow down!" I said, swallowing hard to keep my lunch down. "You're gonna get the cops on us!'

"Probably but isn't this fun?"

"Not for me!"

She laughed even louder and drove even faster, swerving around oncoming traffic and hopscotching around cars moving too slow for her taste.

"For Christ's sake! Slow down! You're going to get us killed!"

"Oh, simmer down, killjoy." She turned to me, her eyes burning. "So, do you have it? The package? That's what Piera's toys were after, right? Oh, tell me we got it before Piera!"

"What? Yes, I have it."

"Wheeee! Open it, open it, open it!"

"Now? Let's wait until we get-"

"NO!" She twisted the wheel, scraping the sidewalk as she turned onto Napoleon Avenue. "I WANT TO OPEN IT NOW!"

"Whoa! Whoa! Okay, okay!" I scrambled to peel the paper and twine off. "See? I'm opening it."

"Good. Just do what I say and everything will be good. Okay? Okay. Open it! Open it!" She nodded obsessively and licked her lips.

I tore the rest of the paper off to find underneath was a simple walnut box with no lid. It was like a solid block of wood. "There's no lid. What is this? How do I open it?"

"Jesus, Giovanna, always playing games. It's a puzzle box, stupid. There's a trick to opening it. Find the bit that slides open the lock. It's usually on the bottom. Just feel for something that moves."

I felt along all four sides, pushing and prodding until I felt something slide and click. The top opened and safely nestled inside the thick cotton was a square, corked bottle about two inches tall. I pulled it out of the box and held the bottle up to the sunlight. A beautiful ziggurat crystal, a rainbow of hues, glittered inside the bottle. It sparkled and dazzled my eyes as the colors bounced from inside.

The dead girl howled in laughter and slapped the steering wheel in victory. "Yes! Yes! And it's all mine! All mine!"

She pulled over and slammed on the brakes. I held the bottle close to my chest and took the brunt of the impact. "Christ! What the hell is wrong with you?"

She put the gear into park, bent over my lap and started rummaging through the bottles on the floorboard.

"Ooof!" For such a tiny thing, she crushed my lap like a cinderblock.

"No, no no! Goddammit! They are all empty!" She popped up and stared wide eyed at me. "Say, you look like a good time guy. Got any hooch back at your place?"

"Yeah."

"Great! Then we can get this party rolling!" She popped the car back into gear and started driving. "Just tell me the way, pretty boy!"

"Fine, just take it easy, okay? No need to get busted by the police. See that street? Take a right down here onto Chestnut and then a left to Magazine Street. I live at 3574 Magazine Street, The Odyssey Shop. Maybe that rings a bell?"

"Odyssey Shop....odyssey....oh! Yes! That's where I..."

Her smile slid away and became slack. Her foot loosened off the gas and the car dropped in speed.

"You died. I saw you. I held you in my arms. And you did you die?"

"Yes. One of Piera's boys jumped me. Stupid thing. It hurt. A lot. It's not the first time." Pain rolled across her pale features, cracking the pretty girl visage. Her foot pressed down heavier on the gas. "I don't want to talk about it."

She looked so lost in that moment, so very young and broken. Her face was so pale I could trace veins in her skin like a roadmap. Her eyes were fixed on the road, but I could see that they were heavy with tears.

"Can I ask a silly question?"
"Fine." She rolled her eyes and sighed.

"Tell me, why a nice girl like you is resurrecting in a place like this?"

She laughed and the heaviness lifted. "You're cute. I like you."

"Want to tell me what you are doing here, playing chauffer, and not at the morgue?"

She shrugged. "Doctors don't always know everything."

"So, you're telling me that you were stabbed a dozen times, carted off to the morgue, woke up and shrugged it off? Does that sum up your day?"

"I also stole this housedress off the woman on the slab next to me but yes, that's pretty much it."

"And this?" I jiggled the shiny crystal inside the bottle. "What is this?"

"The Salt." Her eyes glowed with an insane ferocity and the veins in her face pulsated. "Sal Vitae Aeternam !"

Sal Vitae Aeternam. I did a quick first year Latin translation. "Salt of eternal life?"

"You got it, pretty boy, and, it's all mine!"

Chapter Eight

Between Two Stone Cold Bitches

I asked Pia to park the car down the block and we walked the rest of the way. She seemed to have some difficulty getting out of the car, as if her knees were locking up.

"Are you okay?" I asked.

"Just stiff. No worries!" She smiled, all toothy, but there was fear in her eyes. "Things will be right as rain soon. You got some liquor at your place, right? Whiskey, wine? Anything alcoholic will do."

"Sure, sure. No problem...oh, wait."

"What?"

I didn't need my scars prickly warning this time. The blinds were drawn, and the closed sign was turned round. Something was not right.

"Come with me. Be quiet. We're taking a side route." I took Pia to the patio garden.

"Ooooh, so pretty!" She smelled the flowers and tapped the Elephant Ear plants. "Ha! I like these! So funny!"

"Yeah, yeah. Shhh, Be quiet." Above me was the fire escape ladder. It led to the third-floor balcony that wrapped around the building. We could get to my apartment from there. I put the bottle in my pocket, jumped up, grabbed the ladder and pulled it down. It howled a rusty scream that echoed throughout the patio. I prayed it wasn't as loud as I imagined. "Come on, hurry! They might have heard us."

There was a bit more of a hobble to her gait as Pia walked to the ladder. She grimaced in pain as she reached for the first rung.

"Are you all right?"

"Just feeling my age." She was having a hard time lifting her arms higher than her shoulder. She laughed and started up the ladder slowly. "Promise not to look up my skirt, pretty boy!"

"I shall avert my gaze." I said and I kept my word, mostly, as I followed behind her.

We made it to the third-floor balcony and into the French doors that lead into the front room of my apartment.

"All these boxes." Pia said. "Are you moving?"

"Never really got settled in. Follow me."

She sat down on my bed.

"Well, well. What sort of girl do you take me for? No, scratch that. What was your first clue?" She laughed and went to my chest of drawers. "Ooooh, clothes! Mind if I borrow some?" She let the housedress fall to the floor and stood there stark naked, smiling at me.

She was a pretty little thing. Tight, apricot shaped ass, with hips a man could hook his dreams on. Full breasts that hung like ripe fruit, waiting to be handled, twisted and picked. I could see marbled veins in her pale skin. The only blemishes were strange, dusky patches on her knees and shoulders.

She locked eyes with me, bit her lip and took a step forward. I'm not a fool. Despite the past 48 hours, my body wanted what it wanted. Mea culpa. I reached out for her.

There was a scream from downstairs.

"Shit! Stay here!" I rushed out of the apartment, closing the door behind me and to Bear's office where he kept all the guns and ammo. I grabbed a loaded .38 revolver and a handful of bullets.

I moved quietly to the landing that looked over the shop. I kept low as I tried to get a bead on what was going on downstairs. From my catbird seat, I could see Mama Effie with a busted nose sitting on the edge of her chair, coiled like a viper, staring daggers at a woman in a black, lacey veil, sitting across from her. The veiled woman was Piera. I could see two of the goons I had tussled with back at the alleyway were standing by the doorway. They both were armed with very large, very bloody knives. I didn't see any of Mama Effie's boys lurking around, maybe they ran off when things got heavy...oh, no...wait. There they were. Or parts of one of them heaped up in a corner. I followed a blood trail that led to another grisly stack. I think it was going to take Mikey more than one bucket of borax water to clean that mess up.

Speaking of Mikey...

He was sitting on Piera's lap in one of the comfy chairs Mama Effie's late goons used to keep warm. She had one arm around his middle and a firm grip on the back of Mikey's neck, turning his head, back and forth. She was putting on a show for Mama Effie and Mikey was her dummy.

"Where is Barrington Gunn?" She turned Mikey's head to the right. "Is here over there? No?" A cruel twist to the left. "Is he over there? No?" Mikey cried out in pain, squirmed and Piera squeezed him tighter to her. "Oh, where, oh where can Barrington Gunn be?"

"Leave the boy alone. I told you before..." Mama Effie hissed. "And I'll tell you again....I...don't....know!"

"She's telling the truth." I said. My gun was drawn as I casually walked down the stairs. Piera's boys made a move towards me. "Back off. I saw what bouncing off a brick wall did to your brother back there in the alley. I don't imagine a bullet would be any healthier."

"You destroyed my golem? Well then, you must have some inkling as to what is at stake here."

"I don't know your game, sister, but I do know what you want. And I know where it is. Do I have your attention, now? Let the go of Mikey."

Piera nodded and opened her arms wide. The boy jumped from her lap and ran sobbing to Mama Effie.

"Now, tell your soldier boys to back off."

"Come to me." Piera said. The two men stoically walked over to her and flanked her. They looked like pallbearers caring for a grieving widow.

"You two, get out of here and don't look back. Leave this to me."

Mama Effie gave me a curt nod before rushing out of the door with Mikey. I hastened to the door and locked it behind her. No need for more hostages.

Piera, the veiled lady, sat regally between her two chaperones.

I pulled the bottle out of my pocket and held it up to the light.

She leaned forward, nearly falling off the edge. Oh, she was a hungry one.

"Isn't it pretty?" I said. The nugget rolled around the bottle, reflecting light in a dozen different colors. "Pia called it the Salt of Life. What does that mean?"

"Pia is here?" Piera's voice cracked. She smoothed down the front of her dress. "I heard she was dead."

"She was but you know how flighty she is. Now, tell me. The salt. What is it?"

"It's a long story."

"Shorten it. I don't have much of an attention span."

"These days, my father would've been called a scientist but in 1403, he was an alchemist. After a lifetime of toil, he finally found the Seed, the Salt of Life. Mixed with liquor and ingested, it fixes a person in one state and time. Do you understand?"

I looked at the bottle in my hand with renewed awe. "I think I do. And he gave it to his daughters?"

"No!" Piera laughed, deep and throaty. "Can you believe that he wanted to give it to the Pope? The old man went religious towards the end, exposure to too much mercury, I think." Her veil shook in rage. "We took it from him. Giovanna did, anyway. She snapped his neck like a chicken. Not that I'm sorry. It was our due, our legacy. We had spent our entire lives indentured to that mad old fool. We deserved immortality."

"But…"

"But?"

"There is always a 'but'. This is usually where the 'but there was a price to pay' comes in."

Piera shrugged. "The Salt has great restorative powers but there is a catch. It's not permanent. Every hundred years or so, we need to drink the potion again. There are terrible consequences if we don't take the infusion in time. Giovanna understood it more than I did. She was the scientist. I only dabble with golems and a few toys to amuse myself. Giovanna spent centuries tinkering with the Salt, making it stronger, longer lasting. She hoped to make it irreversible. At least, she did before she changed her mind."

"Why?" I pulled the letter from my pocket. "In Pia's copy of the letter, Giovanna said she didn't want to continue. What happened?"

"Pffft. She fell in love. Can you believe it? Nearly 500 years old and she falls in love. And has a child! Ridiculous."

"Archibald and Arthur."

"They died and she said that life was bland and meaningless without them, blah, blah, blah. She wanted to rejoin them in Heaven. Can you imagine? Heaven! Crazy old woman. But, if that was her decision, so be it. More Salt for me. As long as I have a Seed to grow for the next infusion, I don't need her."

Piera stood up and slipped the veil off. Her face looked like limestone pockmarked by an angry boiling sea. "See? Now you know the whole, sordid story. Happy?"

My hand grasped the bottle inside my pocket. "But what about Pia? Doesn't she need an infusion too?"

"Trust me." She held out a hand. "I will make sure she gets her share."

"YOU LYING BITCH!"

Pia thumped slowly down the stairs, one leg sliding heavily behind the other. Her left arm was frozen in a painful L shape, her elbow jutting out to the side. She was wearing one of my white dress shirts that hung down to her knees.

Piera slammed down her veil and turned towards her sister. "Oh, Pia, sweetie! You aren't looking at all well. You need to take better care of yourself."

"You were never going to share the Salt with me. You sicced your damn golem on me! It killed me!"

"Well, what are you crying about? You obviously got better."

"Ladies! Ladies!" I said, going against my better judgment and stepping in between them, "Stop fighting! You both can have the Salt."

"Why should she get any?" Piera came up behind me and rubbed my arm. I felt her trying to put her hand in my pocket. "Give it to me, Jake. I've spent my life making money. I am extraordinarily rich. I'll make it worth your trouble."

I slapped her hand. "Stop that! There is no need to be greedy. You both need it."

"That little cow would waste it on another life of debauchery and whoring."

"Ha! At least my lovers are flesh and blood, you dried up rock fucker."

Pia cooed to me, "Give it to me, Jake. Afterwards, we can finish what we started..."

"Quelle surprise! There she goes, negotiating with her vagina."

"Oh...you... BITCH!"

And then a lot of things happened very quickly.

Pia screamed and leapt from the staircase. On another day, when most of her limbs weren't turning to stone, she would've made the gap with ease and taken down her big sister with a satisfying body slam. However, today was not that day. Gravity took its due and pulled her cruelly down. I tried to soften her fall, but she twisted and turned underneath me so that when we hit the floor, Pia shattered like a china plate underneath me.

I felt a jagged edge pierce into my gut. It was her arm, stuck inside my belly like a tent pole. Blood rushed out as I pulled it out, unplugging the hole.

But that wasn't the worse thing. Oh, no. Not by a mile. Pia was still alive. And she was wailing. She had split right below the ribcage just enough to give her enough breath to belt out a shrill cry that made my ears ache. Her head twisted back and forth, rocking her against the floor, making more spidery fault lines in what was left of her.

"Piera! Sister! Help me! Please....please....please....don't let me die!"

There were no tears but the pain and fear in her bright gray eyes were enough.

I sat back and did my best to hold my guts in. "For God's sake, Piera, help her!"

"Help her? As you wish." Piera walked over to her sister, lifted her foot, and smashed the heel straight into Pia's face. She did this over and over until there was nothing left but rubble.

"You crazy bitch!" I got to my feet. "You sick, twisted freak."

She snapped her fingers and her golems moved to her side. "Give me the Salt."

"Go to hell. You don't deserve it."

"Please, don't be naïve. She would've done the same to me. She was going to steal it all for herself and you know it. The Salt belongs to me! You're dying and I don't have time to play any more games."

"Games? Okay, you want to play a game?" I held the .38 in a wobbly hand. "How about hide and seek? Start counting."

I took a potshot and hit the golem on her left. I don't know where, I didn't stay to take credit. I hobbled towards utility room and slammed the door behind me.

Chapter Nine

Back in the Utility Room

And this is how it ends for me.

In the back room of a forgotten speakeasy, sitting in a pool of blood, the patsy of a power play between two immortal bitches.

The door is slowly opening, wider and wider, until the hand clutching the knife is now an entire arm with a knife welding hand attached to the end of it. I grunt as I try feebly to push the door. My voice is like a beacon and the knife swipes at my face. I twist and fall on my ass to avoid it. The pain is becoming duller, fading away, like an echo. I'm not sure that is a good thing. I am also having a hard time keeping my eyes open. So tired I'm just so goddamn tired.

And then I feel a pair of strong hands pushing me gently to the side.

"Scoot over, kid. Give an old man some room to work."

I desperately try to see who is there but the flickering light bulbs hanging from the ceiling just make me dizzy or maybe I've gone blind. There is a crack, a thump and a distant wail from the other side of the door as the dark shape shuts the door with one push and locks it.

"Yikes." The shadow bends down and picks the clay arm off the floor. It is sparkling with blue lights that arc off the metal blade as the arm slowly hardens into common clay. "Jesus, it's like holding a live wire. Tickles a little."

My eyes squint and then snap open in recognition.

"Bear?"

"I wonder if I have a place to hang it in the office." He held the arm up as if picturing it like a trophy hanging over his desk. "What do you think, kid?

"I think you're dead, Bear."

"You don't look so good yourself, kid."

I try to sit up straighter but fail. It is just too much work. I slump back down. I don't have much left in me. My hands, arms, legs…feel cold and too heavy to move. Jesus, is this how I go out? Hallucinating? There are worse things to see before dying, I suppose. So, there he is. Bear Gunn. Alive, dressed to the nines, in a hand tailored, Italian three button vested charcoal striped suit made from the finest Merino wool, a flocked fedora, and a goddamn white rose tucked in his lapel.

"Death looks good on you." I say. "Who's your tailor?"

"You can't afford him." He squats, reaches into my pocket, and takes out the bottle. "So, this is it?"

"Yeah."

"Huh. Pretty. Gia kept me on retainer. I never knew why. I just figured it was my natural animal magnetism."

I laugh and then grimace. Laughing hurt.

"Why you, Bear?"

"Why me what, kid? Make some damn sense for a change."

"Never mind. You're not real. It's probably just guilt. My subconscious giving me a chance to ask for forgiveness before I die."

"Forgiveness? For what?"

"For killing you. I'm sorry. Okay? Now.....go away."

I close my eyes, count to three and open them.

Bear is still standing there, tapping his foot. Damn, even his shoes are Italian. Death is a good tailor.

"For Christ's sake. I was good as dead before you found me. You don't have time for all this sissy ass whining."

"So....you are...what? A ghost?"

"I sure as hell ain't your damn fairy godmother."

"Why are you here?"

"Got a job to do. I'm still on retainer and being disincorporated is no reason to cop out on a client. Bad for business."

The banging on the door begins again. It sounds like they had found a battering ram. I am betting odds that Goon #1 is using Goon #2 as the ram. I don't get a good feeling that his career is going to be a long one.

Bear opens a crate and pulls out a bottle of whiskey. He uncorks the bottle with the Salt, shakes the crystal out into his beefy paw of a hand and crushes it. He uncorks the second bottle and carefully pours the Salt into the whiskey.

He corks the whiskey bottle and shakes it vigorously. "Fun fact. Did you know that the Celts called whiskey 'uisce beatha'. The water of life. No joke." Bear uncorks it and hands it to me. "Drink."

I look suspiciously at the dark brown glass bottle. I can't see what is inside, but the bottle feels warm...and it vibrates. It is alive and the smell, oh God, the smell floats on top of the sugary maple whiskey, something like green apples, fresh and clean. It is so, so *tempting.*

"I see it this way, kid. You've got two choices: bottom's up or belly up. Choose wisely."

As if I ever had a choice…

"Bottoms up," I mutter and drink.

The blood in my mouth taints the whiskey with a tinge of copper and I struggle to keep from gagging. It burns, God…it burns all the way down my gullet to my stomach. I stop to take a breath and Bear pushes the bottle back to my lips like a mother coaxing a child to finish taking his medicine.

I finish it up with a few more gulps and then struggle to keep it down. I don't feel anything. I start to wonder if it will seep out of the hole in my gut when fireworks start behind my eyeballs. My brain lights up and burning golden lava pours down my spine, flooding every synapse until every nerve is licked with flames.

My senses explode all at once. I can hear mice pissing in spaces between the walls. I can see shapes and colors swirling in the air, twisting and biting each other, consuming each other and shitting out new shapes and colors. The smells, God, the smells! My nose is assaulted with the smell of decades of stale, old beer wrapped up in moldy paperback books and topped with the jasmine perfume the bitch outside soaked herself in from head to toe. And my skin….God help me….I can feel it bubbling, dying, melting and regenerating. I scream in agony as the hole in my gut turns and twists as my body rebuilds itself from the inside out.

My blood rushes through my veins with the vengeance of Furies. My chest hurts as my heart tries to keep up the rhythm. My cock responds in kind, throbbing with a cold steel erection. All of these things POUND, POUND, POUND inside me until I collapse and explode into a million stars. My entire body seizures in an orgasm and I feel light pouring out of every pore, every orifice as the essence of me is ripped, torn and pulled back together. I am cleansed, rebuilt and reborn.

Minutes, days, hours, years go by as I lie there wrapped up in the afterglow. I don't want it to end. I lick my lips hoping to find just a drop more…nothing.

Damn!

"You…uh…looked like you needed some alone time. You okay?"

"Bear! You're still here!"

"I'm still dead. Where am I going to go? You good?"

"Good? I'm goddamn fantastic! I have never felt better in my life. Let's get to work!"

"Great, kid, but, first…" He picks up a stray rag and throws it at me.

"What for?" I'm covered in blood, sweat and- "Oh."

I do a quick clean up, amazed at how strong I feel, how alive! I can still see the golden outline around my fingers. I check my stomach. Not even a scar. Wait...

I look up at Bear. "I don't have a belly button."

"That's going to be hard to explain to any future girlfriends."

I feel the back of my neck for the puckered circles that branded me since I was a boy. Nothing. I am a blank slate. All the wear and tear on this body from the past twenty-five years in this ragtag life has been erased. And then some, apparently.

The slamming at the door begins anew.

Bear nods at the door. "You ready for some company?"

I jump up to my feet, still amazed at the new strength I feel buzzing throughout my arms and legs. "Sure! Why keep them waiting?"

I wait for Bear to answer with one of his trademark zingers.

"Bear?"

He's gone. Maybe he had never been there in the first place. Grief stabs through the golden rush pumping through my veins. Goddamn, it hurt. I take a deep breath, "Right. No time for that."

I unlock the door, swing it open and step aside as Dumble Dee and Dumbnuts tumble through the doorway and fall on the floor. The one on the bottom, Dumbnuts, has only a nub left for a head and lays still. Good. That was less golem to deal with. His partner in crime, the one who rubbed his head down like an eraser, tries to get up to his knees but I step on his back and push him back down.

"Sorry for the wait, boys."

I smash my heavy shoe into D.D.'s head until I see cracks.

"But I was in the shower and I didn't hear you!"

I keep pounding until I ground his head into rubble.

"NO! You bastard....you son of a bitch....you murderer! WHAT DID YOU DO?!?" Piera screams, shaking in rage. She clenches and unclenches her hands. Bits of her fingers break off with every fist.

I pick up the empty bottle and toss it to her as I step over the rubbish.

"You bastard! You drank it. All of it?" She gasped and collapsed, kneeling. "I'm....I'm finished. Finished..." She rubs the stumps of her hands into her eyes and starts to moan...

And then she starts laughing.

"Ha...ha...hahaha....you   drank   it   all.....idiot. Hahahaha....the seed....."

"What's so funny?"

"You drank it all. Don't you see? You didn't leave any behind to grow for the next infusion. The seed. Hahahahahah! You think you won but...hahahahaha!...you are doomed. Watch me, Jake." She pulled back her veil. The pits were now half dollar sized holes and growing bigger. Her hands were crumbling to dust and her arms followed quickly. " Hahaha! Jake! Watch me and see your fate! Hahahahahah!"

I swear I can still hear her laugh even as the last bit of her crumbles away.

Chapter 10

What the Future Holds

The blinds remained down on the Odyssey Shop for a few days.

Mama Effie came back later that night with a cleanup crew that asked no questions. A mop, a wheelbarrow, a sturdy Hoover and the place was spic and span in a jiffy.

She asked me only one question.

"Is it over?"

"Yes."

She nodded and went back to her register, her universe intact.

I, on the other hand, had a head full of questions and only one person in the world who might answer them.

I searched Pia's car for the wrapper that had the return address from the package.

Three long days of driving in a borrowed car that was running on borrowed time and I found the home of Mrs. Giovanna Lombardi Bonham, wife of Archibald Bonham, a doctor, adventurer and world explorer, mother of Arthur Bonham, a soldier died in Flanders Field, in the

Second Battle of Ypres. I did my research. The detective game wasn't lost on me completely.

The Bonham estate was a large Tudor styled manor on a secluded piece of land surrounded by forests or what passes for forests in the state of Illinois.

I knocked on the door, but no one answered. By the empty feel of the place, I didn't hold out much hope anyone would answer.

I tried the door. It wasn't locked. That did nothing for my optimism.

I went inside, not worrying with leaving fingerprints since they also had been erased.

I walked into the foyer that led to the living room. An ornate, antique grandfather clock tick-tocked in the silence. The weights hung low, nearly scraping the bottom. It had not been tended to in days. It was a beautiful house, tastefully decorated with treasures and keepsakes from all around the world. There were big game trophies, lion, rhino and a Siberian tiger, mounted on the wall.

Above the fireplace, was a portrait of a hauntingly beautiful woman done in the style of one of the Old Masters. If it was of Giovanna, I imagined it probably was done by one of the Old Masters. She had a haughtier expression than her sisters. Her eyes were darker, more intelligent.

Beneath her, on the mantle, were a dozen silver framed photographs of a family starting from the happily wedded couple, to the birth of a new baby, to family portraits of them all, smiling, to singular ones draped with black ribbon. The history of a family from beginning to end.

A French door down the hall, swaying in the breeze, caught my attention. It led to a garden atrium in the backyard. Boxed hedges framed a man-made pond with a mermaid in the center of it, eternally pouring water from a conch shell. Koi fish swam in circles, their scales glittering like gold in the sunlight.

And sitting by the side of the pond, as frozen in time as the mermaid, was where I found Giovanna Lombardi Bonham. She was sitting, cross legged, her serene face looking upwards into the heavens. Ivy had already begun to climb into her lap, darting around her fingers and softly wrapping around her hands like bracelets.

I knelt beside her and looked for answers in her stony gaze. Was she at peace? Did she reunite with her husband and son in the great Hereafter? Or did she simply accept her fate and become cold and dead as stone?

She didn't give me any answers.

I brought her home with me and put her in the patio garden. She is crowned by Morning Glories and good company for the Elephant Ears that Pia admired. I talk to her, sometimes, when I can't sleep. When my head is too full of questions. My Giovanna is a reminder....and a hope...for what lays ahead for me.

In a hundred years or so.

The End

JAKE ISTENHEGYI:

THE ACCIDENTAL DETECTIVE

Book Three

Boodaddies, Bogs and

a Dead Man's Booty

This story is for all the adventurers.

Chapter 1

In the Hull of a Pirate Ship

There are things skittering around me in the dark. I can hear them, splashing and clawing at the rotted wood. They don't scare me. Not anymore. Orange toothed giant rats? Please. Bring them on by the dozen. They aren't pressing the barrel of a .45 into my forehead and smiling about it.

The events leading to this are whirling around my head. A surprise from back home, gruesome murders, Irish gangsters screaming for my blood, and, not least, to end up kneeling in the flooded hull of a pirate ship with the barrel of a .45 in between my eyes. How can so much happen in only four days?

I know one thing for damn sure: that is the last time I answer a classified ad in the newspaper

Chapter 2

"He's the one."

I checked the classified ad clenched in my hand.

'TREASURE HUNTER WANTED. INTERVIEWS ON
FRIDAY, DECEMBER 1 AT LAFITTE'S, BOURBON STREET
AND ST. PHILLIPS. CONTACT W. T. CRABTREE.

SERIOUS INQUIRIES ONLY.'

I stood on the corner of St. Phillip and Bourbon Street and stared at the ramshackle building. It looked like a witch's cottage out of a fairytale. A shiver went through me and I absent-mindedly rubbed the back of my smooth neck. I still expected to feel the bumpy ridges of the circular scars I'd had since childhood. They always twitched before things went pear shaped. Maybe this weird chill was a like a ghost impression?

"Exactly what I need," I muttered. "More ghosts."

There was a shuffling noise as a drunk in a stained coat stumble out of the bar, lean against the wall and spilled his guts on the gray slate sidewalk. It was one o'clock in the afternoon.

"Christ." I shook my head. Dangerous, angry thoughts kept flying around my head, pestering me like horseflies. *How the hell did I fall this far down the rabbit hole??*

Five years ago, I was a stupid kid mooning over a minx who jilted me in Paris. Heartbroken and penniless, I went home to Budapest, hoping to find comfort and was met at the door by my father holding a leather wallet full of money and papers.

"Your Uncle Andor is dead in New Orleans. You are to go there and take over as owner of the building where he kept his shop. Here are train tickets to get you to Germany and plane tickets to New York. You'll be met by a family friend, Greg Desoto, who will get you the rest of the way."

"But..."

"Janos." The way he said my name with such authority mixed with an undercurrent of malice made my blood freeze as a boy. Nothing had changed since becoming a man. My father, Jozsef Istenhegyi, that shadowy figure who pulled my strings, shuffling me in and out of boarding schools, still terrified me. "Do not argue with me. Go. This is no place for a young man."

I didn't even have time to unpack. I did as I always did; what I was told.

In time, I discovered the real business behind the junk façade of The Odyssey Shop. During Prohibition, Uncle Andor had a brilliant plan to make money by letting some industrious businessmen run a racy speakeasy and brothel in the back part of the building behind the bookstore. When Prohibition was rescinded, the party was over, Uncle Andor couldn't settle his bill so he made a deal. In restitution, the building was used by the mob as a shell. To the outside world, it remained a humble, innocent used book and junk store. They played that game for years until Uncle Andor, not a man known for his wits, tried to run out on the bill. He didn't get far before he found himself uncomfortably situated beneath the tires of a bus.

Uncle Andor wasn't only the mob's best customer but was also their public face. Now, there was a vacancy that needed to be filled and quickly.

With the bill in hand, they contacted my father and demanded payment, or they would spell out all my Uncle's debaucheries. As Mama Effie unfolded the story, my bum's rush out of Budapest made more sense to me. While Father Istenhegyi regales polite society of his sacrifice in sending his only son away to avoid being drafted into the

Hungarian National Socialist's war movement, I knew the truth. He needed a sacrifice for his brother's debt. The decision wasn't hard. One bastard half-Roma son in exchange to uphold the Istenhegyi family honor? I doubt he broke a sweat.

Guess who also inherited his debt?

"Twenty-five grand?" I confronted Mama Effie when I found out. "How does one man rack up that much debt in a whorehouse?"

She bristled at the word but kept her cool which caused me more alarm than if she'd smacked me. "He had quite exotic and precise tastes. I could get an itemized list for you if you want."

Mama Effie grinned as my pale face blushed pink. I remembered the explicit murals on the walls of what now is a storage space for the illegal cargo fenced out of the Shop. They served as a menu for whatever sort of physical delight a patron might imagine. The logo on the window outside read, We Go to the Ends of the Earth to Satisfy Your Needs! and the staff of the Odyssey Shop took that boast to heart.

On the upside, in New Orleans I met Barrington "Bear" Gunn, a WWI veteran with gumshoe dreams. He ran his private investigator office, Gunn Investigations, in the apartment above me in the Odyssey Shop. I was his landlord and his sometimes very reluctant partner in crime solving. Most importantly, he was my best friend even though he died over a month ago. I'm the only one that knows because I was the one who put the bullet in his head. Luckily, he doesn't hold it against me.

His ghost is stuck in the Odyssey Shop. If he steps a foot outside the building, he pops right back into his office. So, to keep up the façade, I take care of the office and tell people that he is out of town on a case. So far, no one has questioned although I am worried Mama Effie might be getting curious.

Oh, and on top of my best friend being a ghost, I'm immortal now. Or, at least, I am damn hard to kill.

It all happened shortly after Bear died. I got sucked into a three-way with some psychotic bitches fighting over an immortality serum, the Salt of Life, which their alchemist Daddy had whipped up in his lab a few hundred years ago. The Salt granted the sisters immortality but there was a catch. They had to take a shot of the serum every hundred years. To do that, they had to keep a piece of the Salt crystal, they called it the Seed, to grow and use to make a new batch. The eldest sister, Giovanna, was the keeper of the Seed but she decided to opt out. I guess 500 years is enough for some people.

Unfortunately, the two remaining Lombardi sisters did not share her fatalistic view; each wanted the Salt for herself, leaving her sister to die an agonizing death as she turned into stone. As usual, I was caught in the middle and ended up with my guts ripped out, bleeding to death in the back room.   Luckily for me, I had the Salt. So, I had a choice: take the serum or die.

I drank it and it was like fiery gold ran through my veins. It was intoxicating, amazing. I don't believe there is anything in this world, be it drugs sex or any sort of debauchery that the most expensive whore The Odyssey Shop could dig up, that could make me feel that good again. I still dream of it and, frankly, would do anything to feel that power again. When I came to, I was completely healed. And I mean that in the most extreme sense. It was like I was in a completely new body. No scars, not even my belly button, remained. And the effects have lingered. Now, wounds heal instantly. I've been experimenting, simple stuff at first but I've even gone as far as stabbing myself in the chest. I blacked out and woke up twenty minutes later with only a torn, bloody shirt as evidence. Poisons don't even affect me long. Or alcohol. I can't even stay drunk.

My body metabolizes it before I've had a chance to really enjoy it.

However, immortality isn't all booze and roses. I neglected to leave behind a piece of the crystal, to grow for the next infusion. The question remains: what will happen to me in one hundred years?

That is why I am standing here at Bourbon and St. Phillip, clutching a classified ad and trying to get up the courage to interview for a position. If there is a chance of finding a dead man's treasure so that I can be rid of a dead man's debt, I'll take it.

I took a deep breath, rubbed the brim of my dusky gray fedora for luck and stuffed the ad into my coat pocket. "Once more down the rabbit hole, Istenhegyi."

I crossed the street, sidestepping the vomiting drunk and entered Lafitte's. I had never been inside, but I had heard that it was once owned by the infamous pirate, Jean Lafitte. As to its illustrious ownership I can't swear, but as to whether this building had weathered nearly two hundred years of Louisiana summers, the damp, moldy smell that assaulted my nose was a testament to that much.

There was a low fire in the large hearth even though it was a temperate 70 degrees. On the mantle was a Nativity scene put there, I supposed, to remind the patrons not only of the season but of their Christian responsibilities. Judging by the dozen men drinking themselves into a stupor before dinner, it was a waste of pageantry.

The rough voice of a man shouting, "You're a damn fool, Crabtree!" and the crashing sounds of a table being overturned solidified that thought.

Very few of the other patrons raised an eyebrow as a thick, red headed bulldog of a man broke away from behind the bar. "Look here, Cavanaugh! There won't be none of that here!" he said, pointing a shillelagh towards a tall, unnaturally thin white man that towered over the older, bespectacled, professorial looking man. Next to the older man were two black men, one slim and one thick as a wall, and, beside them, a young woman who, very uncomfortably, stared straight at me.

"Take your troubles elsewhere." the barkeep said.

Cavanaugh straightened and turned to face the barkeep. I swear I heard brittle bones click into place as he moved.

The barkeep hammered his shillelagh in his brick of a hand. "Something you want to say to me?"

Cavanaugh sneered and turned back to the man in the glasses. "You done lost the best digger in New Orleans by listening to this...this witch woman!" Cavanaugh took a step toward the woman and the bigger black man stood up, his eyes bulging in rage. The thinner man stood up, blocking the two men and shook his head.

"Pah! Ain't worth my time." Cavanaugh spit on the floor a great, greasy wad. "The whole goddamn lot of ya!"

He took a wide berth of the barkeep, pushed past me with a gruff, "Pardon" and left through the door I just came in. The barkeep went back to his station and the rest of the patrons went back to drinking.

I stepped up to the group and helped the three men with the table.

"Thank you very much, young man." Crabtree said and held out his hand.

"No problem at all. Are you W. T. Crabtree?" I asked.

"I am. I suppose you are here in regard to the classified ad I posted for the replacement digger?"

"The treasure hunter, yes, sir."

"Well, I hope you didn't travel far, I'm afraid we're not-"

"He's the one," the young woman broke in. "The spirits have spoken to me."

"Him, Pearl? Are you sure?" The slim black man turned to her. "But he ain't even white."

"Excuse me?"

"What are you? Irish?"

"Hungarian."

"Pah. A Dalmatian. Better if he were Irish."

The young woman smiled brightly at me. "He is white enough."

"Okay, I don't need this," I said and tipped my hat to them. "Sorry to waste your valuable time."

Crabtree shook his head and smiled meekly at me. "I apologize, deeply, I do. See, the Baskerville brothers are the best diggers in New Orleans. They've been in my service for years, but they are also terribly-"

"Rude?"

"I was going to say blunt. You see, we follow the old ways of hunting treasure. Spirits, portents, magic. For a group to be successful, it must be racially diverse, you see, to make use of the spirits. Our digger, James, was a white man. We had hoped to replace him with…well, someone of the same bloodline."

"I hope you find someone. Goodbye."

There was a tap on my arm. I turned around and was instantly enveloped in the scent of jasmine. Everyone else in the room blurred into the background. The only face

I could see was the flawless woman in front of me. I willed myself to breathe.

"Let me see your hands," she said, and I gave them to her.

Pearl was a head shorter than me, petite and stunningly beautiful. Her black, wavy hair was long and hung loose down her back. Her eyes were cinnamon brown and looked almost black against her café au lait skin. I felt a stirring inside my chest, something I haven't felt for a long time, at least not since Paris.

She looked at my palms and pursed her lips. "You have no lines. They are smooth, completely blank."

"Oh." I kept my face straight. "I guess I never looked."

She looked up at me through an arched brow. There was a crackling of electricity as our eyes met. "You are a very odd man, Mr. Istenhegyi."

I took my hands away. "How did you know my name?"

She laughed softly and smiled. "The spirits told me."

"I hope they left something unsaid. I'd like them to get to know me a little better."

"Don't worry." She bit her lip and weaved a strand of hair through her long fingers. "They like you enough already."

"So, have you reconsidered?"

I tried to take my eyes away from hers, if only long enough to get some blood to flow back into my brain so I could formulate an intelligent sentence. "Ummmm. Yeah."

"Excellent! Have a seat." Crabtree waved me towards their table. Pearl slid in beside the two other black men. I sat on the other side alongside Crabtree. "First, introductions. I am Wayburn T. Crabtree. These two gentlemen are Thomas and Grover Baskerville. We've been treasure hunting together for years. They have become like family to me." The bigger of the two men, Grover, grinned while his slimmer partner seemed uncomfortable with the compliment. "This lovely lady is Miss Pearl Smith. She is new to our troupe but a most valuable asset. Who do we have the pleasure of meeting and what brings you here?"

I shook my head, trying to push away the fog. "I'm Jake Istenhegyi. I found your advertisement while flipping through a paper. I've never been on a treasure hunt but was intrigued. Who wouldn't be?"

Crabtree chuckled and adjusted his glasses. "No one understands the romance of treasure hunting better than I, Mr. Ist-"

I went to help as he stumbled over my name. I'm used to it. "Ish-ten-hedgy." I said. "Yes, it is a mouthful."

"Well, Mr. *Ish-ten-hedgy*." The slimmer black man, Thomas, leaned forward and pointed a long brown finger at me. "This ain't a game for romantics. There are rules that need to be followed if a hunt is going to yield anything worthwhile. I'm not going out in that swamp with just anyone. Spirits won't lead us right if we aren't pure."

"Pure?"

"Certain things a man has to do to make himself right with the spirits." He began counting on his fingers. "One, a man has to abstain from carnal pleasures. That means no sex."

"Ever? Because…"

"No, fool! Just 24 hours before a hunt." He continued to count. "No alcohol or drugs before a hunt. You must be rested and have a full belly. A man must be devoted to God and, this is the most important of all, his hands must be free of blood. No man who has ever killed will ever find treasure. Spirits will take him down, disgusted at the disrespect if you bring a murderer with you." Thomas Baskerville glared at me like he was looking for a lie. "You all right with all that?"

My stomach tightened at the word 'murderer'. It wasn't murder what I had to do that night in the barn. I had told myself that over and over until it had become truth. Still, I faltered for a brief second until I saw Pearl smile and a wave of peace rolled over me. "Yeah, sure. No problem. My hands are smooth. Ask Pearl."

Thomas grunted and rubbed his Hand of Fatima, a small tin talisman with a delicate black etching of a woman's hand. His thumb shined the tiny turquoise stone in the palm.

"And you are sure, Miss Pearl? He is the one?" asked Crabtree. "We've turned away two dozen men today." She nodded. "What say you, Thomas? You have seniority."

The slim man ran his hands over his talismans, looked down at the floor and over at Pearl. He rolled his eyes and shook his head. "Fine. It's fine by me."

""Excellent! Jake Istenhegyi, welcome!" Crabtree grabbed my hand and shook it like he was pumping for oil. "Our team is finally whole again!"

The slim Baskerville brother drank deeply from his beer mug. The other just stared dumbly at Pearl who smiled brightly at me.

I stared back at her. I felt myself falling deep into her eyes. Swirling, drowning, gasping for air in a cloud of jasmine and café au lait skin.

And down I go...

Stuck

Crabtree invited everyone to his home for dinner to discuss the details for the upcoming treasure hunt. I got his address and promised to meet them all there by 6 p.m.

It was getting close to 3 p.m. when I made it back to the Odyssey Shop so I had a few hours to kill. Mama Effie was in her usual place, sitting high on her swiveled throne behind the register, handing out thick envelopes, whispering instructions to three men in suits and sending them on their way. Her pet goons sat in overstuffed chairs around the bistro table in the corner, reading newspapers or hiding behind them, I was never sure.

I attempted to escape her attention and rush up the stairs to my apartment.

"Good afternoon, *Boss*..."

Her goons chuckled behind their newspapers. She loved to rub it in what a charade it was that everyone thought *I* was the boss.

I stopped on the first step of the staircase. "Good afternoon, Mama Effie."

"So good of you to drop by before closing time. I've got a little assignment for you."

I heard the snap of the envelope that she flapped at me, but I kept going up the stairs. "I don't have time."

"What? This little thing? I'm sure you can squeeze it in while you are out doing Mr. Gunn's legwork."

I took another step.

"Besides, it'll knock a hundred off your tab but, if you're not interested…"

I swallowed down my pride, retraced my steps and reached for the envelope.

She snatched it back. Her ruby red manicured nails flashed as she fanned herself with it. "I heard you were seen wandering around Bourbon Street. Mr. Gunn working a little something downtown?"

"You hear a lot for a woman who never leaves her throne."

She handed me the envelope. It was thick and heavy and taped shut. "Just deliver this to the address on the front."

"I suppose knowing what is inside wouldn't be very healthy for me?"

She cracked a sly smile. "Deliver it at 5 p.m. on the dot."

"Aye, aye, *Boss*."

I heard her mutter, "Damn straight." as I turned away.

I worked off some frustration on the two flights of stairs taking them two steps at a time. At the top, I glanced at the door to my apartment. I finally hired some men to cart off all the boxes and crates that held my uncle's earthly possessions. For the first time since I had come to New Orleans, the rooms were completely cleared of his presence. It was a slightly melancholy feeling. I don't know if it was due to loss or because I had this heavy feeling that I was settling down. The thought of putting down roots made my legs itch.

I wasn't ready so I went back down to Bear's office. His door was closed. I knocked out of courtesy before walking in.

"Bear?" No one answered. The room was empty.

The layout to his apartment was the same as mine. The front half was used as office space for Barrington Gunn Investigations. There was a desk with three chairs on a faded oriental rug he found in a secondhand store. He loved that rug. He said it classed up the place. Beside the door, there were two bookcases full of pulp novels and a file cabinet where he kept paperwork from his cases. The bookcases were crammed full; the file cabinet was mostly empty. He never was one for filling out forms. Bear Gunn was always more of a go out and see what happens kind of guy. It's what got him killed.

His living quarters were separated from the office by frosted pocket doors. I slid one side open and peeked inside. The horrible smell of the pine scented aftershave he exported from England and tobacco slapped me in the face, but he wasn't there.

It was a simple bachelor's pad containing a full-sized bed, a recliner nestled in a corner beside a radio perched on a secondhand table, a shower, toilet and, a small kitchenette. There was a scorched kettle on the hot plate. A plate, a bowl and a cup in the drying rack. Everything in its place, just waiting for the man of the house to come home.

I closed the door, feeling a wave of grief wash over me. God, I needed a drink.

I went to Bear's desk. There in the side drawer were three bottles of Old Forrester Kentucky Straight Bourbon Whiskey. I pulled out a bottle and searched deeper for a clean glass. Instead, I found an unopened pack of Black Jack chewing gum.

I pulled the pack out and snorted a laugh. Bear loved the nasty licorice stuff. He'd chew and then stash the grayish wad under tables, chairs, desks. Anywhere. Here in the office and at Harleux's cottage before she staked him out in the barn to be tortured and torn apart as a ritual sacrifice.

I dropped the package of gum and picked up the bottle. To hell with the glass.

I took a swig and shut my eyes as they teared up, swallowed it quickly, feeling the burn all the way down my throat. I opened my eyes to see a face full of Bear, screaming, "BALOOOOGAH!" as he materialized in front of me.

I dropped the bottle and jumped back. "Jesus! What the hell, Bear? Are you trying to kill me?"

"Figured as long as I'm a ghost, I should practice my haunting skills. Besides, if a knife to the heart didn't kill you, I doubt a quick boo will do the trick. Awww, hell, Jake! Now, look what you did. My best bottle of booze. Wasted."

I picked the bottle up, pulled out a handkerchief and mopped up what little spilled out. "As if you could drink it."

"I can pretend. Besides, look at my rug. I love that rug. It classes up the joint."

"So, you've said."

"Christ, now the place is going to smell like a goddamn taxi dance hall."

"I don't think you can smell, either."

"That's not the point. I'll know it stinks even if I can't smell it." He slumped down in his chair and it creaked in protest. Even as a ghost, the man had force if only in presence. "I'll know it's there and that's enough. I'm the one stuck in here for the rest of forever, Bela."

He only called me Bela when he wanted to cheese me off. One afternoon watching a creature feature with Lugosi and Karloff down at the Tudor and I was tagged forever as Bela. "Don't sulk, Bear. It makes wrinkles."

One good thing, death had done wonders for Bear Gunn's looks. The grizzled WWI vet with gray streaked hair and sagging jowls was replaced with his younger thirtyish rakish young self. Even his wardrobe was now top notch. Perhaps, as a ghost, one appears as one imagines they want to be seen. It would explain his Sam Spade façade. Barrington Gunn was a sucker for the pulp detective fiction magazines.

"Ha. That's the least of my worries." He kicked at the desk, still irritated. "What do you want anyway?"

"I come bearing gifts. I went to the post office." I tossed a stack of letters. "Klaus says hello and asked me to give you this."

I handed him a slab of fruitcake.

"What the hell am I supposed to do with this?"

"The same thing everyone does: ignore it. It's the thought, right?"

Bear snorted out a laugh. "What else you got?"

"Something that will definitely cheer you up…"

I pulled out a film canister from my inside jacket pocket. "I staked out Mr. Jackson like you asked and, bingo! I got him. Meeting up with a young, sweet thing that was definitely not the dowager Mrs. Jackson."

Bear's face broke out in a smile and he guffawed loud and heavy. "I knew that old bastard would break! Excellent! I'll develop the film and…"

His smile faded. The dark room we used was in a friend's apartment.

"But maybe it's best if you develop the photos. Remember how I taught you?"

I nodded. "We should set up our own dark room. I have plenty of room in my apartment."

Bear shook his head. He reached out for a pencil on his desk and picked it up. He held it for a few seconds and then the pencil fell through his hand as if it were fog.

"Sometimes I can hold on, sometimes….not. I can't control it. The last thing I need to be fooling around with is chemicals."

'Okay. I'll take care of the photos." I pocketed the film canisters and waited a beat. "Bear, have you ever heard of W.T. Crabtree?"

"Wayburn Crabtree? I've heard of him. Harmless old guy. Spent last few years looking for Rameau's treasure out in the swamps near Honey Island. Why?"

I showed him the classified ad.

"Treasure hunter? You? Do you know this means leaving the city, right? Out in the muck, getting dirty and pretty much everything you hate." Bear put his feet up on his desk, stretched out the entire six feet four inches of himself and stared at me underneath his thick, wiry eyebrows. He opened the newspaper and read the front page. "This isn't the rag Mama Effie's boys read. Where did you get this?"

"While on the stakeout."

Bear looked up at me under one heavy eyebrow as he waited for more of a story.

"I was down on Canal Street. He was just a dirty bum that crashed into me, dead drunk probably. He was so filthy the he kicked up a cloud of gray powdery dust when he bumped into me. He apologized and slapped at me with the paper but that didn't do much more than get it in my eyes and up my nose. I can still smell it on me. He pushed the paper at me and then walked off. Later, while staking out Jackson, I got bored and glanced through the paper. I saw the ad and figured what the hell. I met with Crabtree and he hired me on the spot."

Bear stared at the tips of his shoes. He was thinking, ruminating on what I told him, and it was making me nervous.

"Is Crabtree still searching for Rameau's loot?"

"I don't have the particulars."

"You don't have the particulars? What the hell does that mean? Jesus, Jake," he tossed the paper down on the desk. "You're just barreling into God only knows what! At least tell me you're packing some heat."

I showed him the pistol in my coat pocket, and he calmed down if only a little.

"I don't like it. Feels hinkey."

"We're going over all that tonight. Look, I know it is a long shot but, damn it, Bear, you know how bad a spot

I'm in. If we strike it rich, I could pay off Mama Effie's goons and be free. I don't want to end up like Giovanna, a shit stained birdfeeder in a patio, stuck here forever."

"Or like me, some dumbass who got shot in the head and is now a permanent resident of the Odyssey Shop."

I felt a punch in the gut as the words came out.

"Bear, you know what I mean…" I checked my watch. "Damn, I need to get going. I have to deliver something for Mama Effie before going to Crabtree's."

"Go on, then. Leave." He picked up the paper, folded it once, twice and then he handed it to me. "What's keeping you?"

He didn't look me in the eye.

Chapter 4

A Sudden Family Reunion

"You have a visitor."

I had made it halfway to the door when I heard Mama Effie call out to me. She pointed a finger towards the patio door. "He's waiting for you outside."

"Who is it?"

"I didn't ask. I'm not your secretary."

My first impressions of my visitor were not good. From the stingy brimmed Fedora, to the gold watch chain that dangled outside his vested gray wool suit, down to the black and white wing tipped shoes, I could smell that this guy was on the make. He was younger by five years or so than me, with a moustache and waxed hair and shoulders so straight and broad you could use them to line up a shot. This was a foreigner trying hard to look like he belonged but the only reference he had was what Hollywood had spoon fed the poor bastard. It didn't help my opinion much that he was stubbing out his cigarette on Giovanna's head.

"Don't do that." I said.

"Oh, sorry!" He apologized and smiled brightly. He had the same sort of quick, charming smile that made more red flags went off in my head.

"I'm Jake Istenhegyi. You wanted to see me?"

"Jake? Jake...." It rolled my name around in his mouth as if he was judging the taste. "Jake. I like that. Good, solid name. American name. It is good."

He spoke with a clipped transatlantic accent, the sort you hear in the movies, like William Powell but there was something else, a familiar sound.

"Your accent. Where are you from? Hungary?" I asked.

"Damn! My cover is blown!" A laugh and smile. "Yes, I'm Hungarian. Roma, actually. More importantly, I am your brother. Well, half-brother." He rushed at me with his hand out. "Radu Tokár."

I shook his hand. "I'm sorry, who?"

He ignored my question and kept on smiling. "So. This is *the* Janos Istenhegyi. Oh, I've heard of you, all my life. Mother never stops talking about her number one son. Yap, yap, yap!" He smirked and his smile faded. "I always thought you'd be taller. Or something. Pity."

His words started to sink in. Mother. Our mother. My mother. The Roma mystery woman that disappeared from my life when I was too young to even remember her face. My last memory of her was tinged with fire and pain. I absent mindedly rubbed the back of my neck.

"I need to sit down," I said.

Radu pulled up a chair and offered me a cigarette.

"No, thanks. Don't smoke."

"You should. It's very American."

"I've been told. Forgive my bluntness but why are you here?"

"Ah, yes." He pulled a very crumpled envelope from his inside coat pocket. "Mother asked me to give this to you. She wants a reply ASAP."

There was something heavy inside. I opened the envelope and shook out the contents into my lap. There was a folded piece of paper, a photograph, and a small, round silver coin. "This is dated three months ago."

Radu shrugged, took a long drag on his cigarette, and blew smoke out of his nose. "Long trip."

The letter was brief and in my mother tongue. Her handwriting was big and loopy like a schoolgirl writing to her crush.

My Janos,

I felt a horrible pain and worried you were in danger. Respond and ease my heart.

Mother

The photograph was of a beautiful woman with dark eyes and wild, curly hair looking over her shoulder. I turned it towards Radu. "Is this her?"

He nodded. "Mother has a vain streak as long as the Danube. You got her eyes. She was always going on and on about that."

I wish I could say I felt something warm and loving but it was like looking at a marquee photo of a movie star. Cold appreciation but no connection.

The coin was silver with an engraving of a circle with an X marked through it, dividing it into four slices. Inside each was a strange squiggle. Outside the circle were more archaic marks. On the backside was a Hand of Fatima with an esoteric eye drawn in the palm.

"What's this?"

Radu snorted out a long plume of smoke. "A protection amulet. Mama is big on amulets, stones, rituals. Look." He tugged on a leather cord around his neck and pulled out a small leather pouch. "She made it for me. It's called a putsi. See? You're not the only one she worries about."

"Obviously."

Radu stuffed the bag back into his shirt and handed me an ink pen. "If you'd scribble something on the back, she'd appreciate it."

I slipped her picture and the amulet into my coat pocket with the film canisters and wrote a quick note letting her know that, yes, there was some trouble a few months back but I came out of it without a scratch, basically a brand new man. The truth in the joke would be lost on her but it amused me.

I gave the letter back to Radu who glanced at it briefly and put it in a stamped envelope. "Nice touch, writing it in Hungarian."

"I haven't forgotten."

"Always the good one." He licked the envelope and mashed it shut. "I plan on forgetting as soon as I can."

"Aren't you taking it back to her?"

"Why in the world would I go back there? I'm in America! No way I'm going back to live in some Gypsy wagon. To hell with that! I'll put this in the post and then my job is done. There is a dark wind blowing back home, brother. Trust me. Hide yourself as far away as you can. Speaking of hiding...."

A cold chill ran through me.

"Can you put your brother up for a few days?"

Chapter 5

Dinner with Crabtree

I was still reeling from the sudden family reunion when I pulled up to the address written on the envelope Mama Effie gave me. It took me to a row of buildings on Felicity and St. Thomas Street. The intersection is in a part of town called the Irish Channel because of the influx of immigrants that settled in the area. Poverty and the stink of cabbage was another reason. Bear hated working the Channel. He would say, "The only thing those damn mackerel snappers love more than drinking is fighting. They'll blacken your eye in the evening and give you a hug in the morning."

There was a band of five boys giving Bear's car a critical eye and calculating how long it would take to strip it. I decided to intervene with some good charity and buy the little bastards off with a couple of dollars to watch my car. One dollar now and one dollar when I returned and only if the car was still there in one piece.

I was looking for a place called Jax. Over a door was a winking neon sign that flickered the word " AX". I guessed the J is silent. It was in a two story wood building that looked like it leaned on the rest of the block to keep it upright. The door was metal and the sturdiest thing about the joint. I knocked twice, the door opened, and jazz poured out into the street.

Ah, that sort of place. Mama Effie, you vixen.

A bald mountain of a man with a shamrock tattooed on the side of his ten-inch bicep looked me up and down. "Yeah?"

I held out the envelope. "A delivery from Mama Effie."

He took it, ripped off the end and flipped through the money. He grunted something that sounded like approval and slammed the door in my face.

"Good doing business with you, too." I said and with that Mama Effie's delivery service was officially closed for the night.

I paid off my delinquent valet service and started towards Crabtree's address in the French Quarter. My palms were sweating. I felt anxious and excited and it wasn't about what fool adventure the old man was planning.

It was Pearl.

If I were totally honest, I couldn't stop thinking about her. I needed to see her. I ached to be close to her.

I'd never felt this way before. And I wasn't sure I liked it.

By the time I parked outside Crabtree's house on Toulouse Street, it was already dark, and I was late. I emptied my pockets of the film canisters and stashed them in the glove compartment. I remembered my mother's picture and amulet and tossed them in as well.

Crabtree's house was a two-story Spanish Colonial that had seen its share of whitewash. The cobblestones that led up to the house were missing a few stones and I feared the porch might fall through as I walked up to the front door. It occurred to me that perhaps I wasn't the only one whose future depended on a big payoff. Bear's earlier comments about things feeling hinkey rang true in my head.

I knocked and Crabtree answered the door wearing a green ruffled apron and holding up a large ladle brimming with what smelled like gumbo. His hand shook and the contents of the spoon dribbled on the floor.

"Taste this. I always worry that I put in too much paprika."

I took the ladle from him and tasted. "No, it's good."

Relief crashed on his face. "Excellent! Come in, come in!"

I followed my host into a large empty foyer. Underneath his apron, he was still wearing the gray striped wool trousers and white buttoned up shirt from earlier but had changed his shoes for comfortable burgundy velvet house slippers. Walking behind him, I took a moment to orient myself. The floor plan seemed simple enough. There was a large empty foyer that led to a staircase. On each side, there were two doors that led to different rooms. Underneath the delicious smell of the gumbo bubbling in the kitchen was the desperate smell of old age and decay, as if the house and the owner were racing each other to see who would cave in first.

"Please, follow me. The others are already here waiting in the dining room." He waved me into the second room on the left. "I'll go check on dinner and be back in a minute. Please sit and make yourself at home, Mr. Istenhegyi."

The dining room was a formal affair. The west wall had three windows that soared to the top of the vaulted ceiling. Red velvet curtains matched the tablecloth. The table had been laid out with white linen napkins, fine bone porcelain china, two silver bowls filled with fresh bread and a six candled silver candelabra as a centerpiece. On the north and east walls were oil painted portraits of stuffy Lords and Ladies that looked down from their gilded frames. To the south was a cherry wood sideboard with an inlay wine rack and four drawers for cutlery, extra linen napkins and sundries. My grandmother had one much like it. Very posh and expensive. The fact Mr. Crabtree had a serving table but no servants cemented my belief that I wasn't the only one here in dire straits.

While Maison du Crabtree was more old money than I expected, I didn't feel half as out of place as the Baskerville Brothers. The skinny one fussed with his bigger brother, making him put his napkin in his lap instead of stuffing it down the front of his checkered shirt. The bigger one just seemed mesmerized by the lit candles. Or perhaps it was Pearl who sat across from them. The flame's glow made Pearl even more spectacular as her light caramel eyes glistened and the auburn in her dark hair dazzled in the golden glow. I couldn't take my eyes off her. My heart began to race, and I felt every muscle tighten at the need to be near her. Damn. There was just something about her that made every atom in me ache.

"Excuse my lateness." I offered an apology as I sat beside Pearl. It was forward, I know, and I saw the twitch in the big one's eye but, damn, if I didn't at least get this close, I was going to burst. "I had to do a favor for a friend."

"Good to see you, Jake." Pearl said, smiling. "I was beginning to worry that we'd lost you."

I reached out for her hand and held it. I felt an instant release in just the touch of her skin against mine. I kissed the back of her hand. "I wouldn't miss this for the world."

She blushed and took her hand back. I turned away and wondered, *what the hell am I doing? That's not me! I would never....what the hell did I just do?* Something about this woman simply melted away all my inhibitions.

I coughed and addressed the brothers. "Hello. Good to see you again."

The skinnier brother nodded and rubbed a talisman as he spoke. He was balding, middle aged and missing two teeth on the upper right side. He wore a white shirt, freshly pressed, with creases up and down both arms. "I'm Thomas Baskerville. This is Grover. He doesn't speak much. I do the talking for both of us."

"Mr. Crabtree told me you were the best diggers in New Orleans."

"I've been working with Crabtree since he got into the game, after his Momma died. How long you been hunting?"

"I'm new to this game. I'm here by chance, actually."

"You must have something going for you," Thomas said, his eyes narrowing as if he was trying to get a bead on me, "if Pearl is vouching for you."

"The spirits are never wrong." Pearl reached under the table and rubbed my thigh. Electricity ran up through my spine. "He has more talents than he wishes to confess."

I reached down under the table for her hand. "I'll do my best to not disappoint."

"Dinner time!" Crabtree burst in and rang a gong, breaking the enchantment. He pushed in a trolley with a silver serving bowl. "It's an old family recipe, Crabtree Gator Gumbo. We like to say, "take a bite out of them before they put the bite on you!"" He laughed and Pearl and joined him out of politeness; the Baskervilles had apparently heard the joke. "Ah, well. Now, if Thomas would lead the blessing?"

Thomas stood up and bowed his head. "Lord Father, Creator of the Universe and all the Treasures in it, thank you for this dinner and bless all those at this table with health and good fortune. In your Son's name, Jesus Christ, we pray. Amen!"

As we all murmured 'Amen', Pearl's came with an extra squeeze higher up my thigh.

Crabtree moved around the table slowly, carefully serving the gumbo. With his palsy, it was a challenge, but I suspect the weight of the silver ladle helped him from sloshing more gumbo into the bowl than on to the floor. I thought about offering to help but the old man seemed to be having too much fun playing Mother and I didn't want to ruin it for him.

He opened a bottle of Bordeaux for those that drank wine. The Baskervilles drank only water.

"Excellent!" he clapped his hands after he finished serving. "Let's enjoy our food and good company. Bon apetit!"

I circled my spoon around in my bowl and wondered which globs were gator. My appetite wasn't helped with Thomas sitting across from me, glaring and rubbing his Hand of Fatima medallion. The big lug next to him, Grover, ate with relish, dipping and rolling his bread into the gumbo and using the roll as a spoon. At the head of the table, Crabtree leaned over his bowl and spooned the gumbo into his mouth with a practiced albeit shaky hand.

Next to me, Pearl ate with delicate grace. I watched her dip her spoon into the gumbo and raise it up to her lips, pink and lush as rose petals, slowly tipping the silver tip into her mouth.

Get a grip, Janos. You're acting like a horny teenager. Christ!

My dinner went cold. I couldn't concentrate on anything but her.

I took a drink of wine and then another until the pulse in my head settled down to a low throb.

"Mr. Crabtree," I asked to break the silent tension, "are these family portraits? You must come from an old New Orleans family."

"One of the oldest." Crabtree smiled. One thing I've learned about my time in New Orleans is that the locals love to talk about their lineage. "It's on my mother's side, of course. Her family bragged that they were descendants from the Le Moyne line. Never had any pedigree to prove it, of course, just these portraits that were handed down from generation to generation. She always moaned how she came down in the world when she married a Crabtree. She fawned over these old paintings like they were her legacy until her dying day. Which was in the room right above us, interestingly enough."

"I'm sorry for your loss."

"What loss? I got this house, didn't I?"

I decided to plug my mouth with a glass of wine before I dug that hole any deeper.

"That's my life story, so, in the spirit of quid pro quo," Crabtree said. "can I ask you something?"

"Certainly."

"I had a quick check done on you and you are not known to anyone in the treasure hunting community, Mr. Istenhegyi."

"True, like I said, this is my first time."

"But you are well known in other circles."

"Oh?"

Thomas Baskerville licked his lips and leaned forward, eager to see if the baited hook would catch a fish. I shifted in my seat and felt for the comfortable, cold bulge of my pistol in my jacket pocket.

"So, I'm left to wonder," Crabtree folded his napkin and placed it over his bowl. "As to why would a private detective want to go mucking about for treasure?"

"I wouldn't know." I answered with a smile. "Since I'm not one. "

"No? You don't work for Barrington Gunn Investigations?"

"No. I rent space to Mr. Gunn. I own the building." Thomas fell back into his seat, clearly disappointed. "The Odyssey Shop over on Magazine Street. Do you know it?"

Crabtree nodded. "I've seen it, walked past it."

"You're not missing much." I laughed and the strange bubble of tension broke. "I know I'm the new kid on the block so I understand you might have questions. We didn't have a proper interview so, please, ask away."

"All right." Crabtree relaxed. "So, what brings you to the world of treasure hunting?"

"Providence? A fluke? Take your pick. I wasn't looking for it. I just saw your ad and thought, why the hell not? If we scored big, it could get me out of a jam. If we don't, I'll still have one hell of a story to tell, won't I?'

"Well, the Good Lord knows how much I depend on His wisdom and the guidance of His Helpers. I believe that Providence brought you to us." Crabtree held his wine glass high in a toast. "God bless!"

Thomas grunted and tossed the remainder of his bread in the gumbo.

The dinner continued but my appetite was shot to hell. Minutes dragged by in silence until a clock chimed signaling that the dinner hour was mercifully over.

"If you would please leave your plates, I'll clear the table later. Now, follow me to the Treasure Room and we can finally get down to business."

Crabtree pulled Pearl's chair out for her and he escorted her out of the room. I started to follow behind them, but Thomas grabbed my shoulder and pulled me back.

"I don't know what you and that little sweet piece of pie are planning," he snarled in my ear, "but I've been working this corner for going on ten years and I ain't in no mind to give it up easy. You tell whoever is backing you two that I was here first."

Before I could retort, Crabtree called out, "Put some mustard on it, boys! We've got a lot to do and little time to do it in!"

"You just tell them that!" Thomas jabbed a bony finger in my chest. "Accidents happen out there in the swamp." he said and shouldered me as he walked past. His shadow lumbered behind him.

I felt a fire burn inside my gut and radiate throughout my veins. I could see Bear's smug face. "Told you so, Bela, told you it felt hinkey."

I looked at the door. *I could bail. I could just keep on walking and get out before I got any deeper.*

Suddenly, the intoxicating smell of jasmine enveloped my senses and she was there, standing in the doorway. Her violet taffeta gown complimented her skin just as much as the plunging neckline, tight waist and flared knee showed off the best of her assets.

"Coming?"

All those thoughts of leaving I had just melted like butter on a hot plate.

I nodded. "I'll follow you."

"Oh, I know you will."

Oh, hell. Here we go.

Chapter 6

The King of Honey Island

One look inside the Treasure Room told me all I ever needed to know about Wayburn T. Crabtree.

Hanging over the thick stone mantle of the fireplace was an oil painting of a huge hulk of a man with black curls underneath a trifold hat, a thick plumed feather and a saucy wench clutching at his thigh. Two pairs of crossed cutlasses adorned each side of the portrait.

There was a tall, locked curio cabinet dedicated to his lifelong pursuit of hunting the booty left by dead men. A strange smell, something like mud and salt water, wafted from behind the glass. I peered inside to see all sorts of strange things, most of them I could barely identify. There were several statues of saints, colored candles, mummified claws of what I guessed were from alligators. There were also bundles of dried chicken feet, the talons clenched in a death grip. Those damned things I knew very well.

Next to it were framed newspaper articles of all of Crabtree's past triumphs. He had found gold in Coillon Island, assorted silver pieces buried near Breaux Bridge and gold coins rumored to be part of Lafitte's loot near Isle de Gombi to mention only a few. In every picture, the

Baskerville Brothers and a strange young man were by his side.

I whistled in appreciation. "You have quite a pedigree as a treasure hunter, Mr. Crabtree. Very impressive."

He waved his soft hand as if shooing a fly. "All in the past. What I have planned will outshine them all! Come, look at what I have set out."

In the center of the room was a round table large enough for King Arthur to pass a keg around to his buddies. There was a large, detailed map for Honey Island, a sliver of land near the mouth of the Pearl River, laid out on the table dotted with red X marks. Most of the red Xs had been marked through with a black streak. Only one red X had a thick circle around it.

We all stood around the table, looking down on the map as if preparing for war. Pearl stood next to me. Across from us the Baskerville brothers stood side by side like a fence. Crabtree was in the middle, like a bridge between two separate islands.

"So, you say you have no experience in treasure hunting, Jake?" Crabtree asked and I shook my head. "Well, I think you will find yourself in a school of a different stripe here. Wouldn't you agree, Tom?"

Thomas Baskerville's lips split into a grin that the Cheshire cat would envy. "I can guarantee it."

I shot him back a toothy grin. "I'm looking forward to it."

"Well, then, for the benefit of our new partner," Crabtree said, "let's start from the beginning."

He walked over to the curio cabinet and swung open the glass doors. The smell of saltwater wafted over to the table. Crabtree bent over and removed a thick, leather journal from the bottom shelf. He grunted as he straightened up. 'I'm not as young as I was when we first started. Isn't that right, Thomas?"

"I hadn't noticed, Mr. Crabtree."

"You are a liar, my dear sir, but I do appreciate the sentiment." He laid the book in the center of the map. There were dull red and blue glass chips and archaic symbols tooled into the leather. "This is the journal of the pirate, Pierre Rameau. He was actually Scottish, the son of a minster, so don't let the nom de plume fool you. He hunted in the waters around the Gulf as well as employed a group of cutthroats called the Chats Haunts as highway men to plague the roads up in Tennessee and Georgia. A nasty bastard and a remarkably successful one. He based his headquarters on Honey Island and where, according to legend, he hid treasures reputed to be worth over five hundred thousand dollars. He was called the King of Honey Island. Hunters have been digging all over that island, looking for treasures and most of them only coming away with hundreds of bee stings."

"Don't forget," Thomas interjected, "the Honey Island Swamp Monster."

"I'm sorry?" I said. "Monster?"

Crabtree waved me away, "I'll get to that in good time." He opened the book. It was a large ledger book with pages yellow with age and faded brown ink. "While we have had several small finds…coins, silver cups, bits and pieces… I had no idea that the jewel of Rameau's Treasure was at my fingertips."

He turned the pages with reverence until he came to an illustration. It was an ornate cross with a bubble in the center. Inside the bubble was a strange looking relic, like a small ziggurat.

"This is a drawing of the Cross of Trismegitus. It goes back to the alchemist, Hermes Trismegitus, heard of him? No, never mind. It doesn't matter. I suspect it is only attributed to him and not actually a relic of the man, if he even actually existed. The cross was carved from a single sapphire. It was about as big as a man's hand. Can you imagine the artistry to complete such a task? Sheer genius. See this in the middle? Yes? That is what makes this such a special piece. It's not just a cross but a reliquary. The legend goes it belonged to a secret society, The Students of Trismegitus, and inside the belly of the cross they kept a crystal called 'the salt of life'. Legend says it cures all ails and to the person who owns it, death holds no sway."

My breath caught in my throat.

The room felt like it was spinning. "And this pirate king, Rameau, he buried it on Honey Island? In a swamp in Louisiana?"

"We've been looking for it for years. These X's mark the spots that the spirits told Thomas and James to dig."

"James?" I asked.

"James Bell. He's the digger you replaced. Poor soul. He died a week ago, hit by a bus."

A chill went through me. I wondered if James Bell had any outstanding debts to the Odyssey Shop.

"And this circled X, this is where you think the Cross is definitely?"

"Yes! All the clues point to it! This was my last chance to find the Cross and leave a legacy. My health."

Crabtree held out his shaking hands and shrugged. "It's Parkinson's. The same thing that took Mother."

"Do you mean to use it to cure yourself?"

"No, son, no!" Crabtree laughed. "I don't believe in alchemy for a second. No, I just want to find it to prove that I haven't wasted the last ten years of my life. Truth be told, I was ready to fold up and die when Pearl and her patron showed up on my door." Crabtree held Pearl's hands up to his lips and kissed them. I felt a twist of jealousy in my gut. "It was a blessing from God, a second chance for me."

"You flatter us, Mr. Crabtree. We helped each other. We had a map that a rival of Rameau's had stolen but it was burned in a house fire so only a third of the original map was usable. We had heard rumors that a journal existed that filled in the blanks. It was a blessing for us that we found Mr. Crabtree."

"See? With the map and the sketches from the journal, there is nothing standing in our way now!"

Thomas coughed. "What about the Honey Island Swamp Monster?"

"Oh, Thomas, don't worry about that!"

"Well, I do!"

"Yeah, let's talk about that. What swamp monster?" I asked.

Thomas pushed the book aside and tapped his finger on the map. "According to lore, Rameau hired a swamp gypsy to conjure up a spirit so fierce and so evil to guard over his treasures hidden all over Honey Island that nothing could face it down. It's supposed to be over seven feet tall, covered in slime and moss, with claws like knives and teeth like a gator."

"And you believe this thing is real?"

Thomas shrugged and Grover's eyes went wide. I could see the little boy inside that huge hulking man piss himself in fear.

"We ain't the only hunters that have spent years looking for the Cross. Lots of other men have gone and never come back. Just as many people have seen it out there. That's why we've always been so cautious. Me, James and Grover, always taking our time and watching the portents. Nothing is worth getting mauled and dragged off by some damn boo hag."

"Which is why now I have a special surprise for you!" Crabtree went to the curio cabinet and pulled out a 5" x 7" wooden box. The smell thickened into a dense cloud as he brought the box closer to the table. Inside were three oyster shells, big gray lumpy stones with sharp looking spikes about the size of my palm. A milky brown goop bubbled from the lips of the shell. When the bubble burst, it was as if the oyster burped, releasing a funk so rotten it made my eyes water. My throat seized and I nearly vomited as we were all immediately overcome by the smell of swamp mud, salt water and rotting weeds.

"Jesus!" Thomas slammed the lid shut. He raced over to a window and opened it. We all followed his lead, gulping in the fresh air. I held Pearl in front of me so she could breathe easier. The smell of her hair cut through the worst of the funk and made me dizzy.

"What the hell was that?" I cried out.

"Boo-daddies. Protection from boo hags, plait eyes and swamp monsters." Crabtree explained. "I had a hoodoo woman conjure up for me. I don't know all the mumbo jumbo that goes in with it but from what I understand, you take an oyster shell and stuff it with marsh mud, Spanish moss, sweet grass and saltwater and let it incubate. She said they had to stay in this box for three days before they would be powered up. If the Rameau's boogie man is what is keeping us from finding the treasure, they are exactly what we need when go looking for the Cross. Honestly, I'm shocked at you, Thomas. You act as if you haven't heard of them before."

"Well, hearing my granny talk about them and seeing them in the flesh is a different thing!" The air seemed to make the foulness thicker. Thomas' eyes were watering so bad he looked like he was a mourner at a funeral. "I can barely breathe for the stink!"

Pearl coughed, held her handkerchief to her lips and she hastened to the door. I followed her and we met outside the house on the porch.

"Are you all right?" I asked. "Can I get you some water? Some wine?"

"No, thank you. I just needed some fresh air." She blushed. "I feel silly now."

"No, I completely understand. No wonder it repels boohags and swamp monsters."

Crabtree and the others came out to the porch shortly afterwards.

"That should be enough for the night." Crabtree said. "They will be ready in two days and then each of you must keep on your person at all times. That is very important. The hoodoo woman said that each Boo-daddy imprints on its master and for it to do that, it needs to lie against your skin for at least 24 hours. I'll need you to come back here on Sunday to get your Boo-daddy. The full moon isn't until Monday. We will meet here at 7:00 a.m.

and, by nightfall, we will have the Cross of Trismegitus! I guarantee it!'

Crabtree bid us good night and went back inside his faded mansion. As the Baskerville brothers pushed past me, I saw pain and confusion in Thomas' face. Grover's remained as flat as slate.

I was left alone with only Pearl. She stood very still, looking at me with those warm cinnamon eyes, as if waiting for me to do something.

"Can I offer you a ride?" I asked her. "Do you have far to go?"

She smiled, took my hand, turned it over and kissed my palm. I felt dizzy as blood rushed from my head. "That depends on you, doesn't it?"

Aw, hell...

Chapter 7

A Night with Pearl

We got in my car and drove a block, a mile, a hundred miles, I don't remember.

She sat close to me, stroking my hair, her jasmine perfume dulling my senses to anything but her.

We pulled up to an address. I don't remember where.

We went inside and fell against the door. Our hands were grabbing, tearing at each other's clothes, stripping each other bare. Our mouths, lips, tongues, hungered, searched and nipped.

A part of me roared and raged to take her, possess her, and consume every piece of her like a lion taking down a gazelle. This wasn't love; it was only lust. If she started crying and pulling away from me, I would not have stopped. The fury and the flame scared the hell out of me but I couldn't pull away.

But her hunger and fury matched mine and she tore into me with as much venom as I had lust. She pushed me onto my back and rode me, snarling and biting into my breast. I arched with the pain and rolled her onto her side and mounted her again. Her fingernails ripped into my ass as she pushed me further, deeper inside with each thrust I wanted to stay there, deep inside her, so warm and wet and never ever ever ever...."CHRIST!" I screamed as I erupted inside her.

She rolled me over on my back, kissed me, covering my lips even though I could barely catch my breath as she slowly lowered herself, up and down on me until I became hard again. She was gentler the second time, just taking her time, using me, up and down, faster and then faster until she arched like a bow, her long hair falling like a waterfall over her shoulders, as she peaked.

And   then....again.   And   again.   And,   oh, oh.....CHRIST...a sharp pain rip through my chest and then everything went black.

Chapter 8

Missing Time and Money

I woke up alone and naked on the floor.

My head was pounding. I hurt everywhere, a deep bone-aching hurt. There was strange red raised welts across my sternum and down my stomach that itched and burned. There were rough abrasions on my wrists and ankles. And I was covered in dried blood. Whose blood? Mine? Oh my God...Pearl's?

I tried to call out for Pearl but my throat felt like I'd gargled barbed wire. I went to the kitchen to get a glass of water but when I turned the spigot, no water came out. I checked the icebox. Empty and unplugged. On the wall there were two buttons for the lights. I pushed and....no light. No dishes or glasses in the cabinets. It was as if no one lived there.

I checked all the other rooms. No sign of her anywhere.

My head spun with exhaustion and confusion. I needed to sort this out but not here. Something deep in my gut told me to run. I found my clothes scattered in the front room. I washed the blood off my face and hands with some water from the toilet tank. I managed to get as respectable as one could with rusty water from a shitter, got in my car and drove home.

It was around 10 a.m. by the way the sun was hanging in the sky when I walked through the door at the Odyssey Shop and the first thing I heard was Mama Effie, squawking like a goose, "Where the holy hell have you been!"

Her voice was like a nail inside my head. "I don't have time for you right now. Out of my way."

One of her goons grabbed me and slammed me against the wall. He pulled my wrist up behind my back and kneed me in the thigh. The ripping of my already overtaxed muscles and the general what-the-hell-ness of my welcome sparked the last bit of fury and I headbutted the ebony son of a bitch, knocking him flat on his ass.

"You want some, too?"

His brother in arms wavered on the sideline as the first goon got up, his nose busted and bleeding. His partner smiled and shook his head as he joined the other.

"What about you?" I pointed at Mama Effie. I was vibrating with rage. "You gonna come at me too, you flat, old hag?"

Mama Effie arched her brow and walked slowly towards me, slapping a rolled-up newspaper against her palm. "Well, well. It looks like our tom cat came home with some fight, didn't he?" Her voice was calm and soft. She stopped an inch way from me and stood there, staring into my face, daring me to make the first move.

I blinked.

She slapped me across the face with the newspaper and then stuffed it into my hands.

"Read the front page, boy, beneath the fold."

Mama Effie stayed in front of me, still as stone. I unrolled the paper and flipped it over. The first headline that caught my eye read, "Body found in Irish Channel". I scanned the story, picking up the highlights. The body of a fighter, Ronan Mallone, garroted, police have no leads, illegal gambling is suspected. There was a photo.

"That's the man I gave the money to. Ronan Mallone. He's dead?"

"Dead as dead can be." A man's lilting voice said. He stepped out of the 'storage room', the illicit back room from where the Odyssey Shop did its real business. He was short, pale and had red hair. Two other men, taller and stockier followed behind him.

Mama Effie's black eyes drilled into mine as she whispered. "That is Dermot Brannigan. Don't be clever, boy. Stand down."

"And you say you gave the money to Mallone?" Brannigan leaned on Mama Effie's counter and polished it with his thumb. "That's interesting because the word is the money never got there."

"I delivered it to the address on the envelope. I gave it to this man." I pointed to the picture in the paper. "Tall, bald, big shamrock tattoo on his shoulder."

"Did you?"

"I didn't get a receipt, if that's what you're asking."

Brannigan laughed.

Mama Effie flinched.

"Receipt! That's rich. I see what you did there." He put his hand out and a man behind him slapped a short, dark, warty stick in his palm. "Because no one does business with the Irish without making damn good and sure," he crashed it down leaving a dent on the counter, "that they get a goddamn receipt!"

Brannigan started at me with his shillelagh held high. I clenched my fist and prepared to knock his red headed block off when a voice thundered from above.

"WHAT THE SAM HILL IS GOING ON DOWN THERE?"

Bear Gunn, all six feet and four inches of him, stood above us at the top of the stairs. Everyone froze as he stomped down the staircase. I wondered if Mama Effie would notice Bear's new look. She kept her poker face stony and her tongue still.

"Dermot Brannigan. You sly slip of a cabbage fart."

Brannigan dropped the stick down to his side and stood tall, thrusting his chin up to add an inch.

Bear stood, toe to toe, and looked down on him. "Do you have business with my partner?"

"Your *partner* failed to make a delivery."

"Jake." Bear's eyes never left Brannigan. "Did you make the delivery?"

"Yes. I gave it to Ronan Mallone at the address on the envelope. A jazz bar called Jax."

"He says he gave it to Ronan."

"Ronan is bloody well dead!"

"Well, that's your problem now, innit?"

The staring contest kept on for an agonizing ten seconds mores before Brannigan broke and turned on Mama Effie. Her pet goons were behind her in a flash.

"I lay this on your head! I want my money as well as 10%...no, you tell them I want 25% interest as compensation for my fighter. You talk to your people. You know where to find me."

Brannigan turned to me. "I'm not finished with you yet, *goulash*."

Brannigan snapped his fingers and his two thugs followed behind him as they left the shop.

"You stupid son of a bitch!" Mama Effie snarled. "What did I tell you? But, no…you had to go and….Sweet Jesus! Where is the money, Jake? Just give me whatever you have left and I'll sort it out."

My jaw went slack. "I swear. I don't have it. I gave it to the man at Jax."

Mama Effie stared at me. "No lie?"

"No lie. Now tell me something: what was the money in the envelope for?"

"Let me take a wild swing." Bear smiled, delighted to be in the game. "This Mallone guy. Irish? Big lunk?" I nodded. "The money was to pay him to take a dive. But, instead, he decided to take the money, win the fight and made a lot of people who thought they had a sure bet very, very angry. Am I close, Mama Effie?"

"Spot on, Mr. Gunn and, by the way, welcome back. I had no idea you had returned. You look…refreshed."

He winked at her. "I feel like a brand-new man."

"Hello! Can we focus on me for a minute? I asked. Mama Effie nodded but I knew this was only a reprieve from her interrogation on Bear. "I delivered the money, but I have no proof. Then the fighter ends up dead. Brannigan thinks I stole the money and killed his fighter. So, what happens now?"

Mama Effie climbed into her beloved seat behind the counter. She rubbed at the dent in the wood and tsked. "If I was in your shoes, I'd buy a ticket out of town and lie low for a few weeks. Let the big boys hash it out. They always do. Once it is all sorted, come back."

"That sounds like a good plan, Jake." Bear said. "You should take a vacation."

"No! No goddamn way!" I was not going to miss out on a chance of getting my hands on just a bit of the Salt. Plus, I had to find Pearl and make sure she was safe. My blood was boiling, I could feel sharp, jagged lightning in my fingertips. "This isn't my fault! I did what you told me to do. If that Mick bastard screwed his own people over, that's their problem, not mine. If they want to try and take me down, let them come. They'll find this *goulash* one hard son of a bitch to put down!"

"Jake." Bear's voice was low. He put his hands on my shoulders. There was no weight, only weird smell of ozone, like when a fuse blows. "Settle down. You're as jumpy as a Chihuahua on an electric griddle. Where were you Saturday?"

"What do you mean? That's today. I'm here."

"Look at the date on the paper, boy." Mama Effie said.

I did. "Jesus, its Sunday. What happened to Saturday?"

"That's what we want to know." Bear said. "What happened? Where have you been? You look like hell. Is that blood under your chin?"

"I can't talk right now."

"Jake…"

"Not now, Bear!"

The red-hot anger that had carried me through was ebbing away and I knew I had to get away before I hit rock bottom. I bounded up the stairs, two at a time and went to my apartment before I did anything that I regretted.

I opened the door and it was as if my uncle's possessions had found their way back home from the dump. The room was littered with boxes and suitcases.

"What the hell?"

"Welcome home, big brother." Radu walked in from my bedroom. Freshly showered, he was wearing my bathrobe and smoking a cigarette. "We're out of coffee and I used up the last of the hot water. What's for breakfast?"

Chapter 9

Bear and Bagels

I pressed my forehead against the shower stall and let the ice cubes beat down on me. The water did nothing for my aches and pain but the chattering of my teeth was shaking a few things loose. It was Sunday?   What happened? Was I drugged? Was it the wine? We both drank it…oh my God,   Pearl. Where did all this blood come from? Was she hurt? I wanted to find her but, damn…I wasn't even sure where to find her.

There was a knock at the bathroom door. "I'm going out. I'll bring back some breakfast. "

"And coffee!" I shouted back.

"Good idea!"

Maybe having a little brother around might work out after all.

I turned off the water and clumsily reached for a towel. I started to dry off when the temperature dropped. Ice formed on the mirror and my breath came out in a cloud.

"So, are you ready to talk…Jesus,   Jake! Who the hell beat you up?"

I whirled with my towel like a matador fencing a bull. "Bear! Get out!"

He put his hands up. "Whoa! Just a welfare check, buddy. You don't look so hot."

"Not now. And not in my bathroom. This is officially a Bear-Free zone. I'll meet up you in your office."

"Fine. You know where I'll be." He said and popped out.

I scraped the frost off the mirror. On my chest, the red welts had become a strange bluish black tattoo that was quickly fading away. It was a cross with a circle, dots and twisted filigree lines. I traced it as it disappeared. I turned to see if I could find more other tattooed marks but all I could find were bruises on my shoulder blades and lower back. There were also scratches across my lower back and bite marks on my shoulders. I remembered the bites most of all. I ran my fingers through my hair and smiled at the memory. And then I got a look at my face. Oh, boy. Dark circles, sunken eyes. There was welt across my throat. I traced it and felt a weird tickle in the back of my mouth. I tried swallowing but the fluttering got worse. It started small, a nagging clump and then it grew and grew until finally I vomited up a great, black ball of greasy snot. It landed in the sink and oozed around the drain.

Christ! What the hell was that?!?

I ran my fingers through my wet hair and stared deeply into the eyes looking back at me. The dark circles were fading, color was coming to my cheeks. My heart was thumping like a jackhammer but I did feel better. I guess it's true. Better out than in. Whatever the hell that was.

I rummaged through my closet and pulled out a long sleeved, off white Henley and gray slacks and dressed.

Radu had settled in by the looks of things. My bed had been well slept in, there were cigarette burns on my sheets and wet towels left on the floor. *Son of a bitch.*

I raided the fridge. I was famished. I guzzled down a cold bottle of beer, pulled out a block of cheese, some bread and ate it like I hadn't eaten in days. Oh, wait, I hadn't.

I checked my watch. It was now noon. I still needed to get over to Crabtree's to get my boo-daddy. And Pearl. He'd know where to find her.

Pearl. What the hell was that about? I have never felt that way about a woman. Total complete obsession. Madness. Yesterday, I wanted nothing in the world but to be with her, inside of her, ripping and tearing…but now, all I really wanted was a cup of coffee.

I rushed up to Bear's office. He was there, his feet up on his desk, sulking.

"Oh, look who has graced us with his presence. Is his majesty ready to entertain visitors?"

"Not now, Bear." I sat down in the chair across from him. My usual place. It was just like old times except now he was dead. "Something very strange happened to me."

Bear straightened up in his chair. "Talk to me. Tell me everything."

So I told him. Starting with the delivery to Ronan Mallone, the Trismegitus Cross, my night with Pearl, walking up naked and bloodied in an abandoned house and ending with the fading tattoo and hawking up a black greasy glob in the sink.

"You got a tattoo?"

"Something like that. It's gone now."

Bear leaned back, stared off into space and brushed his brushy moustache the way he always did when he needed time to think.

After a few minutes, I broke in. "Well? Any thoughts?"

He threw his hands up. "Shit, son, I haven't a clue."

"Great, thanks. Always helpful."

"Hey, this isn't on me, boy. You went out there, jumped in without looking. I told you it was hinkey! Don't put this on my head. How do you expect me to be in the loop now that I'm stuck inside this damn hellhole? If you want my advice, I'd forget Crabtree and all that treasure malarkey."

"And miss out on getting a piece of the Salt? Or money enough to dig myself out of this hole? Are you insane?"

"If it even exists! If you were smart, you'd focus on the little fellas downstairs with the thick, warty sticks. Remember them? They will bash your head in. All you're gonna get running around with Crabtree is skeeter bites."

"I gave the money to Mallone. Whatever happened to it after that isn't my fault."

"You think that bog-trotter gives a good goddamn whose fault it is? You're the last guy to have his hands on the money as far as that little bastard Brannigan is concerned. Shit rolls downhill, Jake. Right now, Brannigan is getting shit on by the bastards above him. So, he needs a fall guy and, hello! I'm looking at him. It doesn't matter if you have the money or if you don't. What matters now, is

Brannigan saving face and if you want to keep yours in once piece, you should get out of town."

"I'm not leaving. Not while there is just a chance of finding a piece of the Salt."

"Then you'd better watch your ass."

There was a knock at the door.

"Hello? Jake? Are you in there?" The door opened and Radu walked in. He had a paper bag and a disposable cup.

"Hello! I am Radu Tokar." He smiled and bowing to Bear. "I'm staying with my brother, Jake, for a few days. Sorry, am I intruding?"

Bear turned to me. "Brother? Looks like you left something out, I think."

"Radu, this is Barrington Gunn. Call him Bear. Come in. Have a seat. Is that my coffee?"

"Oh, did you want one, too?"

"Never mind."

Radu pulled up a chair and sat down next to me. He tore open the bag and used it as a place mat for a bagel and a small tub of cream cheese on the desk. He deftly spread the cream cheese on the bagel and took a bite before asking me, "Oh, did you want some?"

"Never mind."

"So, Radu, Jake never told me he had a brother."

"Ah, well. Half-brother. Same mother, different father. The Istenhegyis don't think too much of my side of the family tree, right?" He prodded me with his elbow. "Janos, I mean, Jake didn't know I even existed until I showed up on his doorstep, looking for a place to stay. Like the hero Mother always told me he was, he took me in, no questions asked."

"Ahhh, is that so? Well, that's our Jake. What a guy. A real hero." Bear's eyes hit me with a look that made me want to kick him. "And are you staying in New Orleans long?"

Radu swallowed and took a drink of coffee. My mouth watered at the smell. "Not long. This is just a quick stop and then I'm on my way to California. Hollywood! I'm going to be a movie star."

Bear's smile grew sharp like a shark's. "Are you now."

"It's my American dream. To be on the screen. I have everything I need, the looks, the clothes, I can sing and dance. All I need is a strong, American name, yes? I've been reading many American magazines... Screenplay, Look, Photoplay, looking for the right, strong, American name."

"Well, I think I can help you with that. See that bookcase over there? I've got tons of magazines with strong American names."

"Really?" Radu dropped his bagel and went over to the shelves that were overflowing with pulp rags.

"Sure! Say, did Jake ever tell you where he got his name?"

"Ooookay!" I stood up. "I'm out of here. I've got things to do. You boys just play nice." I pointed at Bear. "Play. Nice."

"Oh, I'm a freaking saint. I hear I'm best friends with a hero." Bear said as he showed me his pearly whites. "By the way, while you are out adventuring, don't forget the Jackson film. Remember? Needs to be developed? Mrs. Jackson is expecting them on Tuesday."

I mentally kicked myself in the ass. I'd forgotten all about the film. "Sure, no problem. What's one more thing on my plate?"

Chapter 10

Boodaddies and Rubes

In my car, I made a quick search of my glove compartment. Good news. The film canisters were still there along with my mother's picture and amulet. I slipped the photo in my wallet. The amulet was silver. I flipped it, watching it shine in the sunlight. I put it my pants pocket. Call me a sentimental sap. People have called me worse.

Bear had a friend, Frank Weiss, a lonely, retired journalist and photographer, who lived a block away. He rented a flat above a bakery, so it always smelled of fresh bread in his apartment. Bear played poker with Frank and traded his winnings in for time in Weiss' dark room to develop film.

I climbed up the side stairwell and knocked loudly. Frank opened the door. He was a lively little gnome with white hair, a stooped back forever draped in a brown cardigan.

"Jake! It's been so long! I haven't heard from Bear in ages."

"He's out. On a case." The lie was becoming second nature. "He wanted to know if he could pull a favor and get these developed?" I handed him the canisters. The smell from downstairs made my stomach growl.

"Sure, sure, sure. No problem! Can you stay? Have some coffee? I've got some fresh muffins, right from the oven. This will take me a while."

The coffee was the biggest temptation, but I shook my head. "No, I'm sorry. I have an appointment across town. Can I pick up the pictures later today?"

"Sure, sure, sure. No problem. But Bear owes me another game of poker soon. You tell him that. Okay? Two, three hours, tops. I see you then?"

I nodded and gave him my thanks. I made a note to stop somewhere and get the old man a bottle of whiskey for his trouble.

It was around 2 p.m. when I drove up to Crabtree's house. There was a car parked out front, a sleek black Mercedes Benz. Fancy. Not exactly anything I'd figure the Baskerville brothers would drive. I parked behind it and took a quick peek inside the car.

Sitting behind the wheel was a uniformed driver. I tipped my hat to him and he nodded but did not smile. I saw that the interior was clean and well kept. The only thing completely out of place was the small mummified alligator claw hanging from a leather cord on his rearview mirror.

I knocked on the door and Crabtree opened it. "Praise the Lord! Come in, my boy! Come in! They said you'd gotten cold feet."

"Who said that?"

"Mr. Smith and Pearl but, never mind. Spirits don't know everything. I'm just happy you are here. I don't know where we'd get a new digger at this last date. Please, follow me into the parlor."

The room was a simple affair decorated in the taste of local aristocracy. There was a warm fire crackling in the fireplace, two tasteful red velvet padded chairs, a matching Regency sofa and some round mahogany end tables. From the discoloration on the carpet, I could tell that a few pieces of furniture were missing. They were probably sold off to pay for past adventures. On the walls were more oil paintings of dead, dour people that looked down at us as if we had dragged in dog shit on our feet.

"Good news everyone!" Crabtree said. "Jake is here…better late than never, I always say."

"Pearl!" Her back was to me. I rushed to her and turned her towards me. I was so relieved all I took her in my arms and kissed her. She looked up at me with eyes wide with surprise. Something was wrong. This woman was Pearl but, no, not *my* Pearl.

My Pearl, the woman who swirled inside my head, was like a blazing spiral of fire. This woman I held in my arms was cold and plain. Yes, she wore my Pearl's face but with no flair. It was pretty, yes but painfully polite and unpolished. I could see the curves of her hips and the mounds of my Pearl's breasts, but this woman drowned them under beige fabric and large black buttons.

"Hello?" she said, smiling with tight lips.

"Pearl?" I said.

"Yes." She said and shrugged my hands away. She looked towards the man sitting on the couch. The man squinted at her and nodded slightly towards me.

"Oh, yes. You are Jake," she said, apologetically. "Jake Istenhegyi. Yes. Hello."

Even her voice was beige.

"Are you feeling okay?" I asked.

She looked over her shoulder, again, at the man on the couch.

"Pearl?"

"Excuse me. I need to…I'm sorry." and she hurried out of the room.

"I apologize for my niece." said the man sitting on the couch. His voice was a deep bass. "I don't know what to do with her sometimes."

"So true. Who understands the fairer sex?" said Crabtree. "Jake, let me introduce you to Mr. Theophilus Smith, Pearl's uncle and our most generous benefactor. Without him, we would never have this chance at finding Rameau's treasure. Mr. Smith, this is Jake Istenhegyi, our newest digger on the team. You all get acquainted while I go check on our Miss Pearl and see to the refreshments."

I made my greetings and held out my hand. Mr. Smith stared me down as if he were trying to decide which end to start kicking first.

Something about this man made my hackles rise. I knew him but from where? He had a broad face, flattened nose, and lips that I guessed rarely turned into a smile except when sucking on a stogie like the one he was polluting the air with now. He had cropped, wiry hair flecked with gray and his eyes were pale green with gold flecks that seemed out of context with his dark skin. He wore a three-piece suit that cost more than everything I had in my closet. There were gold rings of all sizes on all his fingers and he never stopped twirling his silver buttoned swagger stick. To top it off, hanging from a gold chain on his vest was purple velvet pouch, as big as a fist, with embroidered designs in gold thread.

"So. Jake. Istenhegyi." The way he said my name so singularly and, much to my surprise, correctly, was unnerving. The back of my neck itched, and I resisted the urge to scratch it. "Here you are. Aren't you a man of peculiar talents." He cocked his head, pursed his lips, and then winked at me. "A man of whom the spirits are very protective, yes?"

"That remains to be seen." I laughed out of nerves more than humor. "Will you be going out with us?"

"Good Lord, no! And muddy up my new Italian loafers? No, no, no. That's what I am paying you boys to do. When you reach the station I have, Mr. Istenhegyi, you learn the value of paying others to do your dirty work."

"Still, there is honor in getting your hands dirty in order to get the job done."

His lips curled and smoke rolled out from between his teeth. "Spoken like someone who has spent a lot of time in the dirt."

I finally gave in and scratched the back of my neck.

"Have you been a treasure hunter long, Mr. Smith?"

"Of sorts. I'm a dealer in special antiquities. I have several interested buyers in the Cross."

"Like who?"

"It is the Holy Grail in certain alchemist circles."

"I suppose immortality is a niche market."

"Immortality can be found in a myriad of ways, Istenhegyi, but I am afraid alchemy is not my milieu." Mr. Smith spread out his hands. "I'm merely a facilitator."

"Coffee is on!" Crabtree came in pushing a trolley loaded down with a china cups and a gleaming silver coffee service. "Sugar? Cream?" he asked as he played mother, once again, and shakily poured coffee for each of us. I had never been happier for the interruption.

"How is Pearl?" I asked.

"Hmm? Oh, she was gone."

"Gone? Should we go find her?"

"Don't worry yourself, Istenhegyi." Mr. Smith said. "My niece is a sensitive soul. She probably went for a walk to settle her nerves. Leave her be and drink your coffee before it gets cold."

I took a sip and hid my disappointment. I know that New Orleans prides itself on its strong chicory-based blend but American coffee is bland compared to the Turkish blend my cousin ships me from Szentendre. Still, caffeine was caffeine. I let the wonderful black brew do its magic.

"And before I forget." Crabtree handed me a leather pouch. It reminded me of the one Radu showed me earlier. The smell had died down to a slight air of moldy swamp water.

"It's warm."

"Is it? I didn't notice." he said. "Now, you need to wear it around your neck for twenty-four hours. Keep the bag in constant contact with your skin. That way the boo-daddy will bond with you, understand?"

I hesitated. "Have Thomas and Grover gotten theirs?"

"Oh, yes. Hours ago. Now put it on. Don't worry about the smell. You'll get used to it."

"I'm not so sure about that."

I slipped the soft leather cord over my head and tucked the pouch inside my shirt. The pouch grew hotter as it lay against my skin. "It's burning." I grabbed it beneath my shirt and lifted it off my skin. "Should it do that?"

Crabtree shrugged. "Mine is as cold as a clam. More coffee anyone?"

"Perhaps Mr. Istenhegyi is allergic to your hoo-doo tricks, Wayburn?" Smith said, laughing.

"I don't have much love for any sort of mojo, quite frankly," I said.

"Oh? You are an unbeliever?"

"I've seen enough to never say never but it's only ever caused me trouble."

"You simply have not found the right gris-gris." His fingers tapped lightly on the pouch hanging from his vest.

"True. You are a curator. Perhaps you could help me with something." I fished my mother's medallion out of my pocket and flipped it over to him. "What do you think about this?"

Smith caught it in one hand and looked at it as if a jeweler inspecting a diamond.

"Well, well. What is that?" Crabtree said. "It's beautiful."

"My mother made it for me. Ever seen anything like that before, Smith?"

"Silver. Roma symbols hand carved with an iron nail." He ran his thick tongue over it, popped it in his mouth, and spit it out in his hand. "Traces of blood. Interesting. You have Roma blood then, do you? And your mother made this for you? How very interesting."

Something in the pit of my stomach told me that I just made an unbelievably bad mistake.

He dried it off with a handkerchief and flipped it back at me. I caught it more out of instinct than desire.

He wiped his lips with the handkerchief, carefully folded it and put it in his vest pocket. His gaze stabbed at me, making the pouch on my chest flare up.

"Thank you for sharing. It was quite informative."

There was a ping from another room. "The pastries are done!" Crabtree said, running to the kitchen.

I was left alone, still standing, not invited to sit, and feeling very much on display for Mr. Theophilus Smith's amusement. He looked like a great toad, sitting on a stone, waiting for a chance to snag the hapless fly that landed on the leaf beside him.

To make it clear, that fly was me.

"So, Pearl's your niece." I said to fill the air with words.

Smith nodded and his stare grew heavier.

"Do you think she's coming back soon?"

"No."

He smiled, showing too many teeth.

"Perhaps I should go. Things to do. Big day tomorrow."

"As you will. We'll see you again very soon."

I drained the last of what Crabtree passed off as coffee and bid my goodbyes. I couldn't get out from under that man's gaze quickly enough.

My mood did not lighten as I stepped outside and saw the Baskerville brothers stomping down the sidewalk.

"Hey, you!" Thomas yelled out. "Wait one damn minute!"

Christ, now what?

"Nice car. Belongs to our new boss does it?" Thomas flipped his cigarette and bounced it off the hood. The driver didn't so much as flinch.

"He's inside with Crabtree. Why don't you go in and say hello."

I started towards my car. Thomas stepped in front of me. Brother Grover boxed me in from the rear.

"Why go in when I got what I want right here?" He jabbed a finger in my face.

"What the hell is your problem?" I slapped his hand away.

"You are! You and your Chicago ringers."

"I don't know what the hell you're talking about."

"Don't play smart with me. I've been playing Crabtree for ten years and suddenly some mook out of nowhere shows up with a secret map? Please! Don't insult my profession. I won't rat you out. I just want a cut of the piece. This is the last run for Grover and me. We got to make it count."

. "Are you saying that it's all a con?"

"Oh, *hell*. You're not in the game, are you?" Thomas' eyes grew wide and he laughed. "You're as big a rube as Crabtree!"

"Well, that's not the worst thing I've been called today. Thanks."

"Ha! You stupid shit!"

"Yeah, it was something more like that."

"How about we go get a drink and I deal you in?"

Chapter 11

The Long Game

"It started out as a joke." Thomas picked at the embossed letters on his beer bottle. "Who knew it would last ten years?"

We went back to where it all began, Lafitte's. It was nearly four in the afternoon and the place was crowded. The wind was getting a bit chilly so there was a fire in the hearth. We took a table in the corner, near the heat and where I could keep my back to the wall and my eye on the door. Bear's words this morning to watch my ass had not left my mind.

"Things were hard, no work, no money. We had family counting on us. Me and Grover, we walked all over every parish looking for work. We got a few gigs down at the docks, shucking oysters or doing some construction Uptown but none of those jobs were ever steady. Then one day I hear a couple of guys talking about this rich old coot looking to go treasure hunting on Honey Island. He was wanting to hire some men and he was real particular about what he wanted. He'd found a book on treasure hunting and only wanted men who did it in the old ways. You know what I mean? Spirits, talismans, all sorts of foolishness. I figured, hell, why not me? My granddaddy did a fair amount of digging and so I knew the lore. My great aunt was deep into hoodoo so I borrowed a handful of medallions and beads. I'd play the role of the spirit talker. Grover was our brawn. Then I recruited my friend, James Bell, as a digger because we needed a white man for balance."

"Balance?"

"It's all in the lore. Need to have blacks and whites to do the labor. Don't ask me why. Crazy nonsense as far as I care. Anyway, with James on board, we had a crew.

"Crabtree hired us on the spot. You noticed he's not much for interviewing or getting references."

I nodded and laughed at that. "True."

"It was an easy gig. I'd do the whole boogieman show, shaking, turning back my eyeballs so only the whites were showing, talking to the spirits so they'd tell us where to dig. Crabtree would head out and, surprise, surprise, there was treasure! And not because of some damn spirits, no! Because Grover and James would go out there and bury the damn stuff for him to find. Crabtree would be so over the moon with the little scraps of silver we buried that he never questioned, just paid us to do it again. Like some kid at a carnival, egging on the magician. Do it again! Do it again! So, we hid stuff for him to find."

"And kept taking his money."

"Well, hell! Of course! But it wasn't just that. We kept Crabtree safe from going too deep into the swamp with stories about the Swamp Monster."

"So, there isn't a Honey Island Swamp Monster?" I asked.

"There's something out there, sure as shit, people go missing all the time, I'm just saying it ain't some damn monster made from swamp grass and Spanish moss. More likely it's moonshiners that get nervous about people finding their stills or people getting drug away by gators. Either way, it's no place for a rube like Crabtree to go tiptoeing into, is it?" Thomas took another swig from his bottle and shook his head. "It was a great gig. Everybody was happy, we were making money and then, bam!"

"What happened?"

"That damn Cross of Trismegitus."

"Trismegitus." Grover growled. I was a bit surprised he could speak much less say something with so many syllables.

"So, the Cross…" My mouth was dry, and I took a drink from my bottle. "It's not real either?"

"Could be. History books say it existed." Thomas shrugged. "And it's a part of the lore. See, Crabtree was starting to lose faith. His health was getting worse, with the shakes and everything. He was getting bored with finding trinkets, so I tossed a bigger carrot into the pot. I told him the story just to light a fire under his ass. And it worked! For the next few years, he lived and breathed to find that damn thing. When he came across the journal in an auction in Massachusetts, it was like finding the Holy Grail. I'd never seen him so happy.

"But it didn't last. His body was wearing out. You've seen how he shakes. Well, he could see he was going the same way his mother did and that scared the shit out of him. He started going back down and, well, so did our prospects. So, we convinced him to go all out, one last great hurrah. We figured this would be our last game so we had everything set up. Even had a duplicate cross made up, see?"

Thomas reached into his jacket pocket and pulled out a hunk of blue glass that had been shaped into a cross with a hollowed-out center.

"It's empty." I said.

"Well, didn't want to get too carried away, did we? Anyway, before the hunt, he decided to put out ads, looking for any information about the Cross of Trismegitus. Damn those ads! He's mad for them. We never really worried about the local papers. All the boys here know that Crabtree is ours and they leave him alone. But, damn it to hell, I never thought about him putting one in out of state newspapers. Damn Chicago."

"Chicago." Grover shook his head and pounded the table.

"They came rushing down, Miss Pearl and her mysterious patron. I ain't ever seen him. She's always saying he's away on another business. That something had come up and that he was killing two birds with one stone. "

"I've met him." I said. "If there were birds to stone, he's the sort of bastard to do it."

"Pearl had some half burned up scrap of paper. I never got a good look at it. Hell, he doesn't tell me anything anymore. She sold Crabtree the story that it was a map and that his journal held clues, pieces of the puzzle to find the Cross. Then the three of them started having all these meetings, dinners, and such that we weren't invited to and, before you could count to ten, they had it all sorted it. Where to dig, when to go, everything. If that wasn't suspicious enough, then James got killed."

"That's where you think I came in. You thought I killed James?"

"Not at first. I just thought it was dumb bad luck, him getting crushed by a bus, but when our man was voted down and then you show up out of nowhere...well, you can see how that looks."

"Your man?" My mind went back to that day. "The tall man? Who nearly started a fight?"

Thomas nodded. "Cavanaugh. He's not my first pick, a hot head but, I was desperate."

"And that's why you thought I was part of their plan?"

"Only thing that made sense." Thomas drained his bottle and shook his head. "Now that I know different, nothing makes sense. But I do know one thing," he pulled his boo-daddy out of his pants pocket and tossed it on the table. "I sure as hell ain't carrying this around with me."

I touched the warm pouch underneath my shirt. "Are you pulling out of the hunt?"

Thomas and Grover looked at each other and they both shook their heads.

"I'm a bastard," said Thomas. "I freely admit that before God but I'm not so big a bastard as to leave that poor old coot to fend for himself against two players from Chicago."

"Damn Chicago!" Grover muttered.

"Crabtree is *our* rube and I'm not going to let him get bled dry by anybody but us. Besides, what if they are real? No reason we shouldn't get a fair cut."

"Fair enough." I said. You had to respect a man who knew his own heart no matter how twisted.

"Are you still in?"

I nodded. "Might as well. What have I got to lose?"

As we said our goodbyes and promised to see each other early Monday morning, the Baskerville Brothers walked away a little drunker but lighter in their step. Confession had a way of lightening the soul. The beers hadn't taken much of a toll on my sobriety but, since taking the Salt, nothing did. My stomach was rumbling for something thicker than beer so I decided to see if I could score some grub at Frank Weiss' apartment when I went to pick up the photos.

****

I picked up a bottle of whiskey from the liquor store on the way. The clock was rolling around half past five when I knocked on Weiss' door.

"Who is it?" I heard him say.

"Jake. I'm here for the photos."

There were the sounds of multiple locks being unlatched. That was odd. Frank Weiss was known for his open-door policy especially if you came loaded with booze.

"You okay in there, Frank?"

He opened the door just wide enough to slide a manila envelope through the breach. "Here. I only one roll done. Hope it is enough."

I took the envelope and the door slammed shut. I heard the clinking of locks being turned.

"Frank?" I knocked on the door. "What's wrong? Talk to me."

There was a hesitant pause and then the sound of locks being unlocked.

"Are you alone?"

"Yes."

"Look around. Make sure."

I did as I was told. "There's no one here. Just me. Let me in, Frank. What's got you so spooked?"

He opened the door. The man who stood before me was a mess. His lip was cut and his left eye swollen shut. One of his hands was wrapped up like a mummy. I looked behind him to see his apartment had been tossed around.

"Jesus, Frank. What happened?"

"You! That's what happened." He pulled me inside, slammed the door and locked it.

"After you left, I got to work processing the film and then these two mooks came knocking. They tore up my place, hitting me, over and over, asking me about the money. 'Where's the money? Where's the money?' When I told them, I didn't know about any money, they broke my hand."

"I'm so sorry, Frank. Here, take this." I gave him the whiskey. "It's the least I can do but I promise, I'll find out who did this. They won't get away with it."

"Fine, fine." He opened the bottle and took a great swig. "You do that, Jake, but, for now, get out. Go away. Don't come back!"

I stood outside his door and listened to the locks being slammed into place. I looked around. The street was dark and empty. I hoped it kept that way for Frank's sake.

****

It was close to six when I parked in front of The Odyssey Shop. I pulled the photos out of the manila envelope. In the yellowish glow of my interior light, I flipped through them. They were exactly what Mrs. Jackson needed so she could rip a new hole in Mr. Jackson at divorce court. We could always count on Frank for excellent work. It cut me even harder to realize what he'd gone through tonight because of me.

Then, something caught my eye. Someone in the background. I flipped through the dozen photos and he was in four of them. It was the hobo, the one who ran into me. I opened my glove compartment and fished out a magnifier glass. A weird tremor went through me. He was dirtier and hunched over to conceal his height, but it was definitely him.

Mr. Theophilus Smith.

Chapter 12

Field Tests

The shop was closed for the night so at least I wouldn't have to run the gauntlet of Mama Effie. I wasn't in the mood to fence with her jagged jibes. I wanted to get to Bear's office as quickly as possible, show him what I'd found and get his take on it.

I rushed up the first flight of stairs and found Radu sitting on the bottom step of the staircase that led to my apartment. He was still wearing the smart outfit from this morning although he looked ragged now. His shirttail was hanging out and one of Bear's *Black Mask* magazines was sticking out of his back pocket. He was rocking back and forth; his eyes squeezed shut and he muttered softly over the flame of a white candle.

"Radu, what are you doing?"

His eyes shot open and he jumped up at me, nearly dropping his candle.

"Janos!" He grabbed me by my shoulders. I could feel the heat from the candle on my neck. "Vissza!" *Stay back!*

I broke his grip and took a step back. He was breathing hard and tears streamed from his eyes. I took the candle from him and blew it out.

"Nem!" *No!* He wrestled the candle away from me and struggled with his lighter. "The candle must stay lit!" Once a flame flickered on the wick, Radu relaxed. "It is the only protection we have."

"From what?"

"What's that smell?" Radu wrinkled his nose. "It's like the Danube on a hot day."

"Never mind. Protection from what?"

Radu looked over at Bear's office, turned to me and whispered in my ear. "Did you know that your friend is mulo?" *A dead man.*

"Oh. That." I took the candle, blew it out and opened the office door. "Actually, he is a kisértet." *A ghost.*

"What are you doing? Are you drunk? He's mulo! A curse!" He took back the candle and relit it as he blocked me from going inside. "You will be damned to Hell if you deal with the dead."

I pushed him aside. "My friend, it's way too late."

Radu pulled the magazine out of his pocket and slammed it against the door. "STOP!"

Suddenly, Bear appeared.

"VISSZA!" Radu shouted and shoved the candle in Bear's face.

Bear blew it out, tsked and took the magazine away. "I really wish you'd get your little brother to stop doing that."

Radu screamed, dropped the candle and ran upstairs to the apartment. I imagined he slid a box or two against the door.

"What the hell is his problem?" said Bear. "You know, Jake, behavior like that would hurt a lesser man's feelings."

"What do you expect? Popping up out of nowhere like that."

"Hey! He called me."

"What are you talking about?"

"Come inside." He said, opening the door to his apartment. "Let me tell you about a new ghost trick I learned today."

Bear got comfortable and put his feet up on his desk. He never went beyond the office anymore. What use does a ghost have for a bedroom and a kitchenette?

"After you left, your brother, he is wavering between the names Clifford or Randall right now by the way, and I talked briefly about this and that, nothing in particular really. He doesn't have many interests outside himself, quite frankly. Anyhoo, he asked to borrow a magazine and I told him to take what he wanted and he left.

"I don't know how much later, something weird happened.

"I'm just sitting here, wondering what to do with myself when I felt this tug," he pointed to a spot under his breastbone. "Right here."

"Your solar plexus."

Bear shrugged. "The pull got stronger and stronger and then POP!" He snapped his fingers. "I was suddenly in a shop, surrounded by hats. Radu was there, drumming on the counter with one my magazines, rolled up tight. That man has no consideration for other people's things, by the way. Look at the cover! It's ruined now."

"Are you, what? Connected to these things?"

Bear smiled and shrugged.

"So, if I take one of these," I picked a *Black Mask* magazine out of the bookcase. The cover was of a busty blonde moll holding a bloody knife as her stiletto heel dug into a man's bloody corpse. "You can go anywhere with me?"

"Haven't done any field tests but that seems about right."

"Any *Black Mask* or just these?"

"Ghosting didn't come with an instruction manual, Jake. We'll need to do some field tests."

"Okay, field tests." I sat in my usual seat across from him. "Now, my turn."

First, I told him about going to Crabtree's, getting the boo-daddy and meeting Mr. Theophilus Smith. I glossed over the problem with Pearl; it felt too personal.

Then I told him about what Thomas Baskerville confessed.

"I told you it felt hinkey!" Bear slapped the desk and let out a laugh. "Score one for the old man!"

"Enjoy yourself because you're not going to like what comes next."

I told him about Frank Weiss.

Bear dropped his feet to the floor. He sat up and rubbed my face in exasperation. "Goddammit, Jake...."

"Oh, it gets better."

I showed him the photographs. "These are the photos Frank was able to get done before his visitors wrecked his dark room."

Bear looked and made a whistling noise. "Oh, these are good! Mrs. Jackson will be breathing fire when she gets these."

"That's not all. See that guy in the background? That's the hobo who ran into me on Canal Street."

"So? You think he was tailing you?"

"He's also Theophilus Smith."

"Well, now that is interesting. Are you sure? 100% sure?"

I grimaced. "No, not 100%...more like 98 creeping up on 99. But I'm telling you it is him. I can feel it in my gut. I knew the minute I laid eyes on him at Crabtree's house that I remembered him from somewhere. I just couldn't put my finger on it. He set off all the bells and whistles." I rubbed the back of my neck. "He just felt, well, hinkey."

"And you said the guy before you-"

"James Bell."

"He got killed?"

"Run over by a bus."

"Sounds familiar."

"I had the same reaction."

"This is more reason to go underground, Jake. Take a breather. Just disappear for a while."

I shook my head. "Not with a chance at a piece of Salt. I can't."

"Goddammit, Jake, think this through!"

"I have! Look, I am already one step ahead of Smith. I know that he's not just here for the Cross. Somehow, he is here for me, but the question is why? What would he want with me?"

"Maybe he knew about the Lombardi sisters and the Salt. You said he wore an alligator claw hanging on a chain. Smells occulty to me. Occult type people run in small circles, I bet. Word gets around fast."

"He did mention loas. Maybe he's a rival alchemist?"

"Maybe that's how he made his fortune. Lead to gold. Instant millionaire. Next thing on my list would be immortality."

"Then I need to make damn sure not to turn my back on him. I'm not giving up a chance at finding a Seed, Bear. You understand that, right?"

"You're a damn stubborn bastard. Fine, stick with your treasure hunt but you can't ignore this business about Mallone and the missing payout."

"I don't have a clue where to begin. I was just a delivery boy."

"Then start there. Go back to where you made the drop, ask around, investigate, dammit!"

"Jesus, you're not going to let this go, are you?"

"Nope. And I've got all the time in the world."

All hopes of going downstairs and burying my head under some covers melted away as I walked to the door. "Fine. I'll go to Jax and ask around. I could use a drink, anyway."

"Hey, you forgot something." Bear tossed a *Black Mask* at me. "I'm going too."

Chapter 13

Wakes and Priest Holes

Jax was the definition of a beer joint made flesh. The whole place was a rectangle pit. It was about 18 feet long and 20 feet wide, with long, unfinished wooden shelves on the bare, brick walls and a few three-legged stools. The air was a miasma of cigars, sour beer, sweat, with a whiff of vomit. It was hard to see anything clearly. The three electric bulbs suspended from the ceiling were the only things lighting the dive.

On the bar there were two black draped frames. A photo of Ronan Mallone was in the one on the left-hand side. The second memento mori was of a man I didn't know. The memorials were set as far apart as the length of the bar would allow. The Victrola played "Danny Boy" in the neutral ground between.

Huddled up in two groups were around fifty people, all men with black mourning arm bands. The men on one side of the room glowered at the men on the other. The tension was like a slow growling tiger, pacing through the crowd.

"I don't see Brannigan or any of his thugs." said Bear. "Damn."

"Jesus, Bear, this place is a powder keg, ready to blow. Let's go."

"Hell, no! We're already here. Might as well make the best of it."

"It's a wake, Bear. How do you make the best of it?"

"Trust me."

I'd heard that before. "Just tell me that you have a plan."

As he steadied himself, Bear became even more solid. The air around him got frigid and I shivered. He took of his fedora and smoothed down his hair. "Trust me."

Bear took the first step inside and I squeezed the *Black* Mask in my pocket as if it were a St. Jude medallion. All the faces turned towards us, judging, and waiting to see which side we'd join.   .

We went right down the center and kept walking until we reached the bar.

I felt every eye on our backs, tracing out a target.

The bartender was a thick, black man with a cauliflower ear. He wore a stark white shirt with a blank armband on his left bicep. He was polishing a glass with thick keloid scarred hands. "Which side are you grieving with? Mallone?" He nodded towards the left. "Or Allan?"

A quick nod to the right. "I need to know so as to who to charge."

Every ear in the room strained to hear the answer.

.Bear turned to face the room and leaned against the bar. "Both."

Confusion rippled through the crowd.

"I did not know either of these men. But, as the poet said, no man is an island. The loss of one diminishes us all. Yes?"

Throughout the crowd, a few "Ayes" and "Amens" were uttered as reluctant acknowledgements.

"I'll pay for a round for each party. In honor of the loss of these men."

Normally such a generous offer would be met with enthusiastic yells and cries of 'Good on ya!' but the mood in the room grew darker.

"Keep yer whiskey." A voice from the left said. "I won't be having nothing poured in honor of that bastard."

Someone spit a great gob that landed on the photo of Mallone.

And then keg blew.

"FOR MALLONE!" One side yelled. "FOR ALLAN!" The other chorused and they all rushed toward each other and crashed in the middle with fists, bar stools, swinging belts with heavy buckles and broken beer bottles.

"Ooooh, boy. Get behind the counter, Jake."

He didn't have to say it twice. I hopped over and landed beside the bartender who was already cowering on the floor.

"What about your friend?" the bartender asked.

"He's seen worse."

There was a gunshot and the mirror on the wall behind the bar shattered.

"Goddammit! I told them no guns!"

He tried to stand, and I grabbed his shirt, scrabbling with him. "Keep down! You'll get killed!"

"Get off me!" The bartender pushed me away and popped his head, up and down like a target at Coney Island, shouting, "No guns! No guns!"

A gun flew over the bar and landed at our feet.

"Thank you!" the bartender cried out and slid down beside me.

"I'm Jake, by the way. What's your name?"

"Why do you want to know?"

A chair smashed on the wall behind us.

"I figured it's polite to know who I might die with tonight."

"Desmond."

"Please to meet you."

The roar of the melee continued, and I felt for my gun in my coat pocket. I called out to Bear several times, but he either couldn't hear me over the ruckus or had disappeared, popped back to the safety of the Odyssey Shop.

An idea hit me.

I tugged Desmond's shirt and pointed. "Hey, is that guy starting a fire?"

"What?" He popped up to see over the counter. "Where?"

While he was distracted, I pulled out the *Black Mask* and tapped it against the floor three times.

Bear appeared in front of me, his fist cocked back to deliver a face smashing blow.

"Bear!"

"Jesus, Jake!" He sat back on haunches. He was smiling and angry all at the same time. "Damn! I almost had him! Man! I have never felt more alive! This has been the best night of my life!"

"We have to get out of here, Bear."

"Pffft! This? I told you, micks live for two things: drinking and fighting. They'll settle a few scores, break some bones and tomorrow everybody will be slapping each other on the back."

A half a dozen gun shots rang out.

"That's enough!" a familiar voice called out. "Let's have a little honor for the dead!"

Desmond slid back down. "Shit! It's Brannigan. I owe him two months insurance money."

"Brannigan is no friend of ours either." I asked. "Is there a back way out of here?"

He kicked the cabinet behind us. "There's a priest hole that leads to a secret room."

"A secret room? God, does every building in New Orleans have one?"

"It was a part of the Underground Railroad, and then they used it to hide booze. It leads to the alley out back. Hey, where did your friend go?"

"What? Oh, hell!" I peeked over the bar to see Bear deep in the middle of a fight. Brannigan's bravado did little to break up a good fight. While he was making his way towards the bar, his men were scrambling to pull men apart and get order.

"Ahhh!" I grunted through clenched teeth. I felt a searing burn, like a hot stone on my chest. I instinctively reached for it and felt a lump and realized it was the pouch that held the boo-daddy. I'd forgotten I even had it.

Someone shouted, "DUCK!" I looked towards the sound to see a stool coming at my head. Before I could make a move, the stool swerved as if an invisible hand smacked it away and it smashed five feet away from me. How did that happen? Bear? No, he was still on the other side, punching heads and laughing. I shook my head; a mystery to solve at another time because, right now, Brannigan was staring straight at me.

"You! GOULASH!" he shouted and picked up his step. Luckily, he was slowed down by a clot of fighting mourners.

I slid back down to the floor. "Brannigan saw me! Bear will have to catch up."

"For the best, I guess." Desmond said as he opened the cabinet. Inside was a priest hole, about 3x5, with a ladder that led down to God only knew where. "I doubt he could've fit anyway."

Chapter 14

More Pieces of the Puzzle

"Go! Now!" Desmond hissed and I didn't question. I slid, feet first, down the hole and felt for the rungs. The ladder was surprisingly stable so I had no problem climbing down and landed on the dirt floor below. I looked around but couldn't see anything in the gloom. The air was musky with the smells of wood, booze and mold.

Desmond followed and once he was a few rungs down, he reached up and slid a panel over the opening and secured it with a metal slide lock. With our only source of light gone, it was now completely dark.

"Looks like you've done that a few times." I said when Desmond landed next to me.

"Not my first time at the rodeo." He picked up an oil lantern and lit it. "Watch your head. There ain't much overhead."

He wasn't lying. I bent myself into a L-shape and tried to keep in his footprints.

"So, tell me the truth." Desmond said. "What in the holy hell were you and Bear Gunn trying to accomplish up there?"

I smacked my head on the ceiling in surprise. "Ouch! You know Bear?"

"I know about everybody that comes and goes. People don't take much attention of me, not since I had to step away from fighting. People think I'm a meathead, that my brains is scrambled because I took a few hits too many. Ha! It didn't do my ear no good, Lord knows, but my brain is fine. Besides, I got another ear. I hear stuff. I listen and, most important, I remember.

"Are you all looking for the missing drop money?"

I was too tired to try and play cool. "Yes. We know that Mallone was paid off to throw the fight but Brannigan claims he never got the money. Mallone didn't throw the fight and now lots of people are out of money and he's dead."

"Well, it sounds like you got a few pieces right but that ain't the whole story."

"Fill me in, Des. My ass is riding on finding that money."

"Scuttlebutt has it that Mallone was all set to throw the fight. Why wouldn't he? He got paid, right? More green in his pocket for less punches to his mug. And everybody knew how much he loved his mug. He was a ladykiller. Oh, yes. Not a skirt in the Channel that Ronan Mallone hadn't had a turn under, so I hear.

"Now, the other fighter was supposed to be Martin O'Reilly but when Mallone got in the ring, he was facing Fergus Allan."

"Allan. He was man in the other frame."

"Yep. He died this morning. Scuttlebutt has it that Allan paid off O'Reilly and Katzimmer for the chance at Mallone because Mallone had taken favors from Rosie, Fergus' wife."

"Wait." My head was spinning trying to keep up with the playlist. "Who is Katzimmer?"

"Joe Katzimmer. Mallone's manager. He took the drop off payment from Mallone. I saw that with my own eyes."

"So, Katzimmer took money for Mallone to throw the fight and money from Allan so he could settle a score? He got paid twice for one job. Sounds like a good gig. What soured it?"

"Scuttlebutt has it that Allan didn't know about the fight being rigged and went in swinging, fists and teeth, at Mallone. Well, you can see what sort of position that put him in, right? He didn't have a choice but fight back or Fergus Allan would've killed him."

"It was self-defense, then."

"That's not how Brannigan and his boys see it. All they see in the bottom line, the bets that went sour and the face they lost. So, I figured Brannigan killed Mallone."

"But he didn't; Brannigan thinks I did."

Desmond stopped suddenly and I almost ran into him. "Did you?"

"No. I delivered the money, but it never made it to Brannigan. He thinks I stole the money and killed his fighter. He's looking to take it out of me to settle the score."

"Well, well, now that answers a question that bugged me all night." He stopped at a stone staircase. "Here we are. This leads to an alleyway. From there, we go our separate ways."

I shook his hand. "But first, tell me the question that bugged you."

"All those people that came tonight to give their respects, they were friends, family or other fighters." Desmond shook his head and smiled. "I kept asking myself, where the hell were Mallone's manager and Allan's wife?"

Chapter 15

Katzimmer

I made it to my car just in time before New Orlean's finest pulled up with a paddy wagon, ready to crash a few drunken Irish heads. I drove away as nonchalantly as possible, just another law-abiding Joe, thank you Mr. Police Officer, no, nothing to see here, until I got a block away and hit the gas.

I drove until I came to an all-night diner called Sunnyside. I parked, pulled out my *Black Mask*, and tapped it three times on the steering wheel.

Nothing.

I tapped it again, harder.

"Jesus, Jake…" Bear was hazy and faint, like a negative that had gone through the wash too many times. "What do you want? I'm knackered. I'm-"

And he was gone to wherever it is that ghosts go to recharge. I was my own to find Joe Katzimmer.

I went inside the diner and found a public phone booth. I squeezed into the tiny closet and closed myself inside. The phone book was hanging from the wall on a chain. I sat on tiny stool and searched for Katzimmer.

Luck was still on my side. There he was: Joseph Katzimmer, 1610 Constance Street.

It was a fifteen-minute drive. There were few streetlights in this section of town and my headlights cut through the dark like a dull butter knife. One house had numbers on the mailbox, and I counted down to Katzimmer's.

I parked three houses down from his address and walked back. The houses were of the Shotgun type, one story and long and thin, like a dog run for people. They were pressed close together, maybe only six feet of grass between any of them. Only one window glowed with light and, as my luck held out, it was Mr. Katzimmer's house.

The window was on the side of the house. I peeked inside. It looked like a living room. There was a radio, a couch and framed prints of faded flowers on the wall. I could hear a man talking loudly. I tried to open the window just an inch so I could hear better. Yes! It slid up easily.

A woman entered the room. She was a mousy little thing with straight, dull blonde hair and a thin, pinched face. She was wearing a pale-yellow dress and fiddling with a long pearl necklace, threading it around her fingers. Her face flittered between anger and boredom as she sucked on a cigarette.

A man followed her.

"You can't walk away, Rosie! Nobody was supposed to ...I never signed up for anybody to die."

As plain as she was, he was twice as ugly. Short and squashed like a toad in a suit, he had no neck to speak of, shoulders that rested beneath his ears and long arms that ended in square, beefy hands. He wore a terrible toupee to hide his receding hairline. He scratched at it with yellowed fingernails. He was wearing boxer shorts and an undershirt that strained against his beer belly. He was pale and shaky like a drunk who hadn't had a drop in too long.

"You got the money you wanted, didn't you?" Her voice was high and annoying.

"Well, yeah....but-"

"But what, Joe?"

"It wasn't supposed to go down that way. That wasn't the plan. I had no idea they changed the roster. Mallone was supposed to fight Marty O'Reilly. Who in their right mind would pit him up against Allan? Everybody knows about the trouble he had with Fergus ever since...well, you know. Nobody would've put those two dogs into a fight and expected either of them to not fight to the death. I can't keep this money now. It's wrong. It's blood money, Rosie."

"So, give it to me." She took a long drag off the cigarette and tossed it out the window. I dodged the red ember and thanked God she didn't think twice about an open window. She pulled her pearl necklace over her head and palmed the strand with a practice hand. She turned away from the window. I saw him pass the envelope to Rosie

"It's not as if it's your hands with blood on them, anyway." She said as she counted the bills and stuffed the roll into her bosom

"For God's sake, why, Rosie? Why did you have to go and do that for? Mallone didn't know. He wouldn't have told nothing."

"I did it for us. He was so jealous and when he saw you with me...doing what you were doing to me..." He licked his lips as she traced his face with her fingertip, "We couldn't take that chance."

"But now Fergus is gone too...you have to believe me. I had no idea! No idea, hand to God! This has all gone screwy. I wish to God you had never put that idea in my head. I wish I'd never listened to you, Rosie!"

"Don't say that, sweetie. You're all I have left in the world."   She pressed his face against her breasts and wrapped his long arms around her and kneaded her ass with his hands.

Huh. So, that's why they missed the wake.

She patted him on the head. "Joe, honey, be a lamb and bring me a drink, sweetie. Please?"

"Sure, sure. Anything for you." He went in for a kiss which she deftly avoided.

"Drink first. Sugartime later."

The little man turned and waddled away. In a flash, Rosie held the pearl necklace tight in both hands and swung it down, over Joe's face and under his chin. She pulled up hard, yanking him off his feet. He struggled, kicking and losing his footing, falling to the ground. She fell on top of him and kept pulling the necklace, as if they were reins on a bucking stallion.

"Holy hell!" I pulled out my pistol, ran to the front door, kicked it in and rushed to where they were. Rosie was gone and after a quick check on Joe, I found out he was gone too.

On my knees, I got a better look. The poor bastard's face was purple, and his tongue jutted out of his mouth like shoe leather. She had twisted the garrote so viciously the pearls had embedded into the skin of his neck.

"What we do for love, right, Joe?" I said as I closed his eyes.

I felt the cold barrel of a .38 kiss the back of my neck.

A deep baritone voice whispered in my ear, "Ain't that the truth, mister."

So, my luck finally ran out.

"Put your hands up."

I obeyed.

"Well, look what you got here." He took my pistol away from me. "Rosie! Rosie! Get your sweet ass in here and see what I caught!"

"What are you going on about? Oh, well...." Rosie came in and walked over to me. She bent down and stared at me with cold, granite gray eyes. There wasn't a grain of sanity in them. She rubbed her nose against mine. "Hello, there." she said and kissed me.

"You know this loser?"

"Not yet but he's cute." She kissed me again and turned her attention towards Joe's body. "Oh, I almost forgot my babies!" She started untwisted the garrote, pulling the string of pearls out of the fold of his neck. When she finished, she put them in her pocket and skipped back to the man holding the gun at my head.

"Let's take him with us." she said.

"Why not just kill him here?" he said

"He can be our new toy. Come on, Judd, it's a long drive to California." she said.

"Do I get a say in this?"

I heard the click as he pulled back the hammer.

"No."

I closed my eyes and waited to see if a bullet in the head would be enough to kill me for good...and then I felt that horrible burning on the center of my chest.

"What the hell is that? JOE?! Oh my God....JOE!"

Before I had time to react, cold hands pushed me to the side as a shot went off right by my left ear, deafening me.

What happened next was terrible enough to watch. I'm grateful I couldn't hear the screams or the sounds of Joe's corpse tearing Judd's arm off and then clubbing him across the face with it. Blood splattered across Rosie and her face tore open in a scream. Joe grabbed her by her hair and slammed her down to the ground. He put one foot on her chest, twisted the hair around his hand and yanked until her scalp tore off her skull. He then started stomping down in the center of her body. She curved up like a bow, blood spurting out of her mouth like a geyser with each push of his foot.

Judd was crawling towards me with his one good hand. I hadn't gotten good look at him until now. He was handsome, movie star handsome. Everything Joe lacked, this stud had it in spades. Thick dark hair, blue eyes, muscular with a chiseled jaw. He was mouthing out words I couldn't hear but the terror in his eyes was all I needed to know he was begging me for help.

I shook my head.

His face twisted with anger as he clawed at me and screamed, "You bastard!"

I didn't need ears to hear that.

Joe straddled over Judd and grabbed his movie star face with both hands and PULLED....back...*hard*. His head snapped back like a candy dispenser. Gristle popped out and hit me in the face and then blood covered me like a fountain.

The only one left was me.

I spit and gagged as I crab-scooted across the floor, slipping in the gore, stopping only when my back slammed up against a wall. Joe took two steps towards me and then another two. He stopped in front of me and cocked his head, his engorged purple tongue flopped to the side like a

Labrador retriever and then…he dropped. He folded up like an empty suit at my feet.

I felt a piece of me shut down, but I didn't have time for that. *"Get it together, Janos! Get the money now, fall apart later."* I slapped myself across the face. Twice. Each time, harder.

I was running on automatic. I stepped over Joe's body and stumbled over to Rosie. I did my best to not step much of the gore that had splashed around her and took a deep breath before I plunged my hand into what was left of her chest cavity. I fingered around until I felt the roll of money. I tugged it out from between some rib bones and put the roll in my pocket. I picked up my gun beside Judd and finally allowed myself to breathe as I got in my car to drive back to the Odyssey Shop.

But, first…

Chapter 16

A Few Brief Stops

My first stop was Mama Effie's house. I don't know what shocked her more. Me showing up at her doorstep covered in gore or the fact I knew where she lived.   The second one, more than likely.

It was near 10 p.m. and she answered the door sans makeup, her hair in rollers and in her bathrobe, defenseless.

I dropped the bloody roll of money at her feet. "Joe Katzimmer stole the money. Rosie Allan killed Mallone. They are both dead now. Tell Brannigan we are square. If he has any questions, tell him to talk to me and to leave my friends alone.

"And, before I forget, have your boys hose out the car when they get to the shop. It's a mess."

I didn't stay to hear her reply.

****

My next stop was to see Frank Weiss.

I knocked on his door. "It's Jake."

I heard the clink and clank of several different locks. The door opened as far as the chain on it would allow. Frank's eyes, bruised and scared, peeked out.

"It's over. No one will hurt you again. I promise."

He nodded and closed the door. I only heard one lock turn and that was enough.

****

I parked around back of the Odyssey Shop. I emptied my pockets. I put my wallet, some change, my mother's amulet and my gun on the hood of Bear's '38 Packard. I stripped down to my boxers and tossed the rags in the backseat. Mama Effie's boys would know best how to deal with them.

Crabtree's mojo bag was still hanging around my neck. The leather pouch was clean, completely untouched with blood, like a circle of white surrounded by muddy red. The bag felt light and warm. I thought about tossing it in with the clothes but something about that felt wrong. There was more to this bag of oyster shell and swamp weeds than met the eye… or nose.

I'm not sure how but this bag saved my skin twice tonight. I owed it some respect.

The night was cool but I was so tired, I was beyond feeling the cold. I walked around to the patio and gave Giovanna my customary pat on the head, not giving a damn if someone saw me walking around in my skivvies, a wallet in one hand and a gun in the other. This is New Orleans; they've seen weirder. I jumped up, hooked the fire escape ladder with my wrists, pulled and climbed up to the balcony outside my apartment.

I walked into the front room via the French doors and kicked over a bowl of water. What the hell? All the lights were on. There were candles and more bowls of water everywhere. There were white lines of salt near the windows and doors.

I heard someone walking in the other room. My grip on the pistol tightened and then I remembered. Oh, yeah. Radu. My half-brother and sudden roommate. Was the salt, candle and bowls of water some Gypsy way of keeping Bear, the big bad boogieman ghost, out of the apartment?

I didn't know and was simply too tired to care.

"Radu? Come here. We need to talk."

He walked into the room with his hands up. His bruised cheek and bloodied nose told me all I needed to know. Brannigan came in with him and three other mugs rolled up behind them making it a real party. I couldn't see but I figured the little bastard was holding a snub nosed gun tight up against Radu's kidneys.

My gun hand went up instinctively. "What the hell, Brannigan?"

Brannigan laughed. "I could ask the same, Goulash. Not exactly dressed for the occasion, are you?"

"It's been a long night." I put my gun hand down. My arms were shaking with fatigue. I couldn't have kept up the façade if I wanted to anyway. "It's over. I found the missing money and gave it to Mama Effie. You'll be hearing from one of her boys soon."

"Will I now? And where was it, pray tell?"

I didn't have it in me to tell the whole story, so I just pointed out the highlights. "Joe Katzimmer palmed it. Rosie Allan killed Mallone."

"Is that right?"

"Did you hear me? There is no reason for anyone else to get hurt. It's all sorted."

"You'll understand if I need more proof than just your word."

"Christ, Brannigan! Look at me. How much more sorted does it need to be?"

He pushed Radu to the floor and stormed at me, gritting his teeth.

"I don't like you, Goulash." He put the gun to my gut. "You don't show the right sort of respect."

I felt the pouch grow warm.

"Ever been gut shot? It's a nasty way to go. All your innards spilling out on the floor. You never can get the stain out."

I grabbed the pouch, now hot to the touch. It vibrated in my palm. "You really don't want to do that."

"Who's gonna stop me?" He pushed his mug up into mine. Thick, rummy cologne scraped the inside of my nose. "You? Unless you are hiding something I can't see in those boxers, I think you are outnumbered."

Pale, dull animal stupidity stared back at me. Brannigan was never going to let this go. It would be easier to end this now.

"So be it."

I released the pouch and the temperature in the room dropped a few degrees. The electricity prickled against my skin as the Boodaddy gathered up energy to strike.

"Hey, Boss!" a voice called from behind the door. There was a knock. Three sharp bangs and two softer ones. A blonde headed man came in and gave Brannigan a note to read. I was impressed with how little his lips moved.

He folded the letter and put it in his pocket. Brannigan stepped back, holstered his gun and snapped his fingers. "Roll, boys. We're done here."

The temperature of the room went back to normal.

"I have one last thing, Brannigan."

He slung the word at me. *"What?"*

"Some of your boys roughed up an old man tonight. Frank Weiss."

"So?"

I took a deep breath and tried to be as intimidating as a man covered in blood and wearing boxers could look. "Lay off my friends. If you want me, *come get me.*"

I smiled and hoped the gore staining my teeth relayed the message with even more panache.

He slammed the door to let me know it was.

When we were finally alone, Radu picked himself off the floor. He was pale beneath his bruises, shaking and looked as if he was going to puke.

"Janos….tessék! I mean…" he sputtered. "What the hell?!?"

"Let that be a lesson: there are worse things than having a kisértet living below you. "

"Are you bleeding? Where did you get all that blood?"

"It's not mine. Now, get out of my way. I need a shower and God help you, there had better be hot water."

"Yes, yes. I am sorry but can I ask one more question?"

I sagged with exhaustion. "Make it quick."

He reached out to touch my navel free stomach and I slapped his hand away. "Is that an American thing?"

"Yeah." I said, walking away. "It's an American thing."

Chapter 17

Nightmares

I showered and crawled naked into an unmade bed. I slipped the boodaddy off and put it under my pillow. I think it needed the rest as much as I did.

I glanced at my alarm clock. I have a chance at catching five hours of sleep before I needed to be at Crabtree's.

Easy enough if it weren't for the nightmares.

I kept seeing Joe in his death throes, the pearl necklace biting into his neck, his purple tongue hanging out of his mouth like a leather strap. Except, in the dream, Joe changed places with Rosie. He was strangling her but it wasn't her, it was Pearl. And it wasn't Joe standing behind her, it was me. Her fingers scratched at my hands, tearing them apart and making it harder to grip the bloody strand. And then she changed into Henrietta Harleaux, the bitch who had served up Bear as a sacrifice. My hands were smeared in blood as I pulled the pearl necklace tighter and tighter around her neck. And then we switched. Henrietta was standing over me. She was just as beautiful as when I first saw her. Flashing green eyes, mocha skin and long, lush hair. She twisted the bloodied strand of pearls tighter and laughed like a maniac as I struggled to free myself. My fingers slipped over the slick pearls as I choked and nearly bit my tongue in two trying to breathe. My chest burned as if a knife were burning circles and lines into my skin. In the dream, I felt myself losing control. I was dying. Can that happen? Suddenly, there was a woman's voice calling out my name. "Janos! Janos! Védje meg!" *Protect him!* and then a green, brackish wave came from nowhere and washed Henrietta away from me. I could hear Harleaux screaming out curses as the waters drowned her away.

I woke up gasping for breath. My body felt like a tenderized slab of meat hung on a hook and left for coyotes to chew on. The alarm clock warned me I had two hours to get myself together. I lied there, flat on my back, for a few minutes, closed my eyes and just as I felt soft sleep wash over me, Joe's distorted face, his leathery tongue flopping wildly, would crash through and I'd wake up, my heart beating against my ribs.

Sleep was not in the cards so I settled for another shower. Extra hot.

Chapter 18

The Precipice

Time was dripping slower than a broken faucet. I had hours to kill before heading over to Crabtree's house so I went upstairs to Bear's apartment. I was anxious to fill him in on what had happened after the pub last night and catch him up on the details.

I knocked twice and went inside. The apartment was empty. Not the kind of empty one feels if a room has been left vacant but the sort where it feels like something had been scooped out, leaving a hollow shell behind. I called out for him but no response. I thought about rolling up a *Black Mask* magazine and trying out his new ghost trick, but something stopped me. What if he didn't pop up? What if he'd worn himself out like a light bulb and was now out for good?

I went back downstairs and worked on walking a groove into the floor. At times like this, I wished I'd taken up smoking. Hell, why not start now?

Radu was sleeping on the couch. I rummaged through his coat pockets.

"What are you doing?" He sat up and asked.

"Starting a new hobby. Where are your smokes?"

"Sorry. I'm out. Went through an entire pack thanks to last night's excitement. Why are you up so early?"

Radu was this far in, I decided he might as well know the rest of the story. I left out the Sisters and the Salt. No need to let all the cats out of the bag.

"Pirates? Here? That's incredible. Can I come? Please? What a story that would be to tell people in Hollywood."

"No deal. There are too many wild cards in this deck as there is."

"Please!" He got off the couch, went to the tallest of his wardrobes and opened it up. It was jammed packed with clothes. My jaw dropped; my closet barely has enough clothes to get me through the week.

"Why do you travel with so much..." I flipped through some blouses, jackets and three taffeta gowns. "...stuff?"

"You never know what a part might call for. I must be ready for anything. Ah, here it is! I have an authentic French Legionnaire's uniform with pith helmet. I won it off an actor in New York who had been an extra in an Errol Flynn movie. It would be perfect. Please?"

"No. Radu, trust me on this. You need to get out of here; get on the road to Hollywood as soon as you can. This place has a way of sucking you in."

"Fine. As you wish. I'll leave today. I'll be gone before you get back. Promise."

"Good. It's for the best."

"But, as a parting gift, let me do one little thing for you."

What does one wear to go treasure hunting? I'm not an outdoorsman; I prefer the feel of concrete beneath my feet and tall buildings looming over me to dirt and trees. Nor am I a clothes horse. A life of being shipped around boarding schools fostered a philosophy of traveling light. I was pleased when Radu offered to share with me from his closet even if his pool of practical knowledge was colored by what he's seen in movies. I chose to wear a pair of heavy boots, sturdy khakis, a long-sleeved Hensley and a safari jacket over his choice of a French Foreign Legion uniform complete with a pith helmet. The sand colored jacket had an amazing number of pockets which made it easy to carry my wallet, my mother's talisman, my pistol and a very crinkled copy of *Black Mask*. I slipped the boodaddy over my neck and tucked it under my shirt.

We shared a final cup of coffee before I left to go to Crabtree's. It was strange. I think I might miss him.

****

I pulled up to Crabtree's house. The only other car was the Baskerville's truck.

"Good morning!" Crabtree called out from his front door. He was wearing a white linen suit with WWI combat boots. "Come in! Come in! We have so much to do!"

Seeing Crabtree in his choice of adventure wear cemented the wisdom of my choice.

"I have laid out a nourishing breakfast for us to enjoy before our journey!" Crabtree said as I followed him into the Treasure Room. "Please, make yourself at home and eat. I'm much too excited."

There was a banquet table of food, pastries, juices, fruits and, best of all, coffee. Pearl was already there, spreading raspberry jam on a piece of toast.

She was dressed much the same as me in khaki trousers, sturdy boots and a loose blouse. She had her hair secured in a bun that nestled on the nape of her neck. She wore only a dusting of blush and a touch of lipstick. She looked very pretty. Almost the Pearl I remembered from our night together but more real, more solid.

I sat down next to her and she shifted her knees away. She continued to look at the floor.

"Listen, I feel badly that we haven't been able to talk since..." My mind searched for an appropriate word to describe the last time we were together. "Dinner. "

Her eyes cut over at me. "We have nothing to talk about."

"Please, Pearl, we need to talk about Saturday."

She crossed her arms across her chest. "What about it?"

"Mainly, what happened to it?"

She cocked her head to the side. "You don't remember?"

"Well, of course, I remember some things. Quite a lot of things, actually."

She blushed. "I can't help you."

"There is this hole, a complete void. It's as if I ceased to exist for an entire day. What happened?"

"Please, stop."

"I woke up alone, covered in blood. I was scared to death something had happened to you."

"Stop it." She wilted and turned away and whispered. *"No. Please. Not now."*

"You act like you don't even know me. I can't tell if you are angry or…" Just then another option occurred to me. "…are you scared of me? Why?"

Suddenly, she straightened and rose like a cobra. That fiery wildness I remembered was back in her eyes. She leaned forward and put her face so close to mine I didn't know if she was going to kiss or bite me. *"Istenhegyi! You bastard! Why can't you just stay dead!"*

"Jesus!" I pulled away from her. "What is wrong-"

A bass voice pulled her back. "Pearl."

It was her uncle, Theophilus Smith. He shared the same sense of fashion as Crabtree, dressed in a cool linen suite although minus the combat boots. The strange purple velvet pouch swung on the belt at his side which was a bit jarring.

"Pearl, is this man bothering you?"

Her rage drained away instantly, and she swayed as her voice trembled, unsure. "Uncle?"

"What have I told you about talking to the help?"

"Pearl, come into the parlor, please."

She rushed past Thomas Baskerville as she followed her uncle.

"And good morning to you too, Miss Pearl," he said as she walked away.

Thomas grabbed a bagel. "Women, huh?"

"Women." I walked over to him and grabbed an apple. "That's the truth."

He called over to his brother. "Grover, come over here and show Jake."

The huge man nodded, opened his shoulder bag, and showed me the fake Trismegitus Cross.

"Grover did a little something extra to it last night."

"He put a crystal in the center."

"It's Old Crabtree's last run. We didn't want him to be disappointed if this goes tits up."

"I wish someone had my back like that." I said and bit into my apple.

"Look, it ain't none of my business but," Thomas took a long drag on his cigarette, "if that Pearl were my woman, I'd keep my back to the wall and a hand over my balls."

"Balls." Grover echoed and nodded.

"There's something…twisted… about her."

I rubbed my chest. "It might be too late for that."

****

We left Crabtree's house in separate cars. The Baskerville brothers had a beat-up Ford pickup truck. The original black was now spotted with frequent blemishes of rust. I helped them load the back with shovels, tarp, rope and a toolbox Thomas called his gris-gris kit. He winked when he said it now that he knew I was in the game. I patted the boo-daddy nestled under my shirt and nodded.

The rest of the crew rode with me. Crabtree sat shotgun, perky as a Labrador puppy going on a car ride, and Mr. Smith and Pearl sat behind me. I could feel her eyes drilling into the back of my head.

We rode that way for nearly ninety minutes. I followed the brothers' truck as they took the newly finished Highway 90. Crabtree filled the silence with all the minutiae one could stomach about the history of the building of the highway. His voice became a droning buzz within ten minutes, and I let my mind wander.

What was wrong with Pearl? I couldn't get a bead on her. I'd never swear to be an expert on women but, damn! And what about Pearl's uncle, Theophilus Smith. Was that him in the photograph? What did he want with me? It didn't fit. The unlikable, posh, three button vested suit man I met in Crabtree's parlor was not the sort to go slumming on Canal Street. For that matter, what made him change his mind about coming today? He was more concerned about mucking up his loafers than finding the treasure just one day ago. What changed?

"Over fifty men died making this highway." Crabtree's voice drifted into my thoughts. "My barber, have you met Saul? He works at a shop near Royal, he said he was told that they were tributes, sacrifices to the spirits of Lake Pontchartrain but he's the sort to throw salt at a black cat. Still, he gives a damn fine close shave..."

And what happened to Bear? During the pub fight, it was like he was his old self, alive and roaring. If you didn't know better, you'd never guess he was dead. Maybe he was like a battery. One that blows out now and then and the Odyssey Shop was where he recharged. My heart hurt to think he was snuffed out. It was selfish but I didn't want to lose him. He was my only friend.

"I remember when this was all lake. Just water and more water as far as you could see. The only way to get anywhere was to wait for a ferry or hire some dreadful flatboat to cross it. And in the summer there would be awful mosquitoes big enough to carry you off. My mother always claimed her poodle, Peaches, was snatched by the skeeters. Ha! She never found out that it was me that left the gate opened. I had to line the sidewalk with food before the stupid thing made it out into the street. Sweet Lord, how I hated that dog..."

And what to do with Radu? He promised to be gone by this evening. I need to get him out of New Orleans before he spills the beans to Mama Effie...

I clenched the steering wheel at the thought.

If he talks to Mama Effie, things could get very complicated. Very, very...complicated.

Still, if this turns out good, if we do find some anything valuable out there, I could make enough money to pay off Mama Effie, and, what the hell; I'll go with Radu to California. I'm not making any new friends in New Orleans especially now that I'm on Brannigan's wrong side. Bear can come with us. I'll take a whole library of Black Masks if that is what it takes. And, of course, there is the Cross of Trismegitus. If there is a sliver of Salt that I can use in a new elixir, all my troubles will be gone. Poof, like a magic wand!

"...and then I told the police it was just another boy spouting lies, trying to make trouble...why are you smiling, Jake?"

"Sorry. Just thinking."

****

We caught up with the Baskervilles at Caudill's Dock. The air smelled of wet blankets and fish. The bare cypress trees that bordered the swamp looked like sharp, grasping fingers scratching against the silver sky. I could hear the chittering of birds but could not see them and things skittered and splashed into the water. I would see them just out of the corner of my eye but never straight on. I missed the solid pavement of Bourbon Street. Drunks I could handle but invisible things that crept and crawled beneath bushes? No, thank you.

A tall lanky man with the name Paul embroidered on his shirt walked over and shook Crabtree's hand. "I got her ready, just as you asked. All stocked up and ready to go."

Crabtree pulled out his wallet and slipped a wad of cash into Paul's hand. "I'm sure you did. Tell your missus I said hello and I'm looking forward to having you both for dinner very soon. Promise to bring your instruments and I'll make my mother's famous jambalaya."

"Much obliged." Paul tipped his hat. "The missus has been nagging me for new violin strings. I'll pass on the invite."

"Now that, my friend, is a boat." Thomas Baskerville smiled wide, showing all the gaps in his teeth. "Where in the world did you conjure up such a beauty, Mr. Crabtree? You been holding out on us?"

I wouldn't know a beauty from a beast when it came to boats but, even to someone as clueless as me, it was impressive. It was about fifteen feet long, six feet wide, and room for ten people. *Precipice* was painted in golden letters on the dark oak hull.

"What are those circular pits on the front?" I asked.

"Oh. Gunners cockpits." Crabtree said. "Or where they would be if we had them. Merely decorative, I'm afraid. This is a prototype for some boats I recently acquired from an old friend of mine. He is trying to sell the plans to the military. The final product will be larger, sturdier and, according to Higgins, will win wars. I don't know about all that but I do know it can go anywhere in the swamp you need to go. From depths to the shallows, *Precipice* can get you there."

"What's that small cabin near the front? An outhouse?"

"That's the wheelhouse, where we steer and control the boat. Sweet Lord, you are green!"

As I watched the boat bob up and down in the current, I guessed I would be feeling very green very soon.

"Come on, Jake." Thomas slapped me on the back. "Time to finish loading up."

"No, not you." said Smith, shaking his head. He pointed at me. "Only him."

"What? Are you joking? We'll get done in half the time if we all do it."

Smith and I stared at each other.

"The spirits demand it."

"So that's how this is going to play?" I rolled up my sleeves. "So be it."

"Take off your jacket," said Smith.

"What?"

"And your shirt. "

Thomas winked. "He's got a point. Sweat offends the spirits. All part of the lore."

"Lore." Grover said, a smile splitting across his face as he sat down.

"Unbelievable." I took off my jacket and shirt and handed them to Thomas. "Hold this. And I know how much is in my wallet so don't get any ideas."

"You still wearing that thing?" he pointed at the pouch around my neck. "Rube."

"Shut up."

Thomas laughed and sat down beside his brother. "No worries. We'll supervise, ain't that right, Grover?"

"Huh. Supervise."

I ignored their supervision and loaded up the boat. It took around an hour and then we were ready to head out.

"It's done." I said as I dressed and checked my jacket pockets to make sure nothing was missing. "Let's get going."

"But, first." Crabtree said. "Thomas, if you would do the benediction, please."

"Right, Mr. Crabtree." Thomas crossed his hands over his stomach and bowed his head. We all did the same. "I call upon St. Christopher, be with us as we travel these new roads. I call upon St. Anthony, guide us as we search for things that are lost, I call upon the Loas Brigette for luck, Damballa, Father of all Creation and Erzulie Dantor as a protector for all those upon the good ship *Precipice*. Hear me and guide us to the treasure that we seek as we have followed the old ways and purified ourselves. We have not drunk spirits from the bottle. Is that right?"

"Amen." Everyone muttered despite the fact whiskey rolled off Thomas from three paces.

"Nor pleasure of the flesh. Is that right?"

"Amen." Pearl squirmed a bit at that one.

"And no one in this circle has the Mark of Cain? Our hands are pure and never spilled blood?"

The group said in unison, "Amen!"

"Istenhegyi?" Mr. Smith asked.

My tongue felt like wet clay stuck to the roof of my mouth.

I swallowed drily. "Sorry, yes. Amen."

"Amen!" Crabtree shouted. "Pearl, my dear, take my hand. It is always good luck to have beauty go before age."

The rest of the crew followed behind them. Thomas and I sat on wooden benches on the left and Grover sat across from us on the right. Smith, Pearl and Crabtree, went inside the wheelhouse. He pulled a cord and a siren blared out causing a flock of birds to shoot out of the trees, squawking and pissing as they took flight.

"Hold on!" Crabtree called out. "Fortune and glory await us, and the Precipice is ready to take us there! Onward, HO!"

He slowly reversed, hit the dock twice, stopped and sputtered before getting the *Precipice* out of the harbor. The brown, murky water was inches from the... port? Starboard? Bow? I don't know....just that it was damn close to being inside the boat where, frankly, I'd prefer it stayed out.

Something bumped the side of the boat. What was that? A rock? A log? A fish? Do fish get that big? I leaned over to see what I could see. Just muddy water. I reached out and dangled my fingers in the water. I

Thomas leaned over to me and whispered, "I wouldn't. Gators hide out on the bottom. Might confuse your wiggling fingers for fish. Snap them right off." He winked, leaned back, and settled in for a nap.

Did I mention how much I already missed Bourbon Street?

Chapter 19

The Hidden Fork

There was a primordial aura about the swamp, a feeling that this land was untouched and the water never sullied by boats. There were patches of shade on the water where Cypress trees towered over us, blocking out the noonday sun. The sawgrass that grew on the banks were so thick as to be an impenetrable wall. Beyond the sawgrass, there were tall elephant ear plants that swayed back and forth, even though there was no wind.

"What's that?" I pointed to the moving plants.

"Could just be wild pigs." Thomas said. "Or rats. Big ones. The size of a dog. They are all over these swamps."

"Swamp rats?" I remembered Moe warned me about swamp beavers and now there's rats?

"Story goes that some hat makers decided to corner the beaver market by breeding some big assed European rats called nutrias. Then the stock market crashed, the hat market dried up and those poor bastards were stuck with a ton of rats that nobody wanted so they dumped them in the swamp thinking they'd be gator bait. Turns out they were wrong. Sons of bitches are everywhere. We can't kill them quick enough and not enough gators to eat them all."

"Good to know. Gators, pigs and giant swamp rats. All my favorite things."

"Uh-oh." He pointed towards the wheelhouse "Something is going down. Follow me."

Thomas knocked on the panel above the door. "What's the problem, boss?"

"There is some confusion about the map." said Pearl.

"The map shows that there is a fork in the river, right ahead of us." Crabtree turned the wheel to the left and revved up the engine. "We are to take the left branch and follow until we find the hidey hole of the Pirate Pierre Rameau!"

The river ahead of us took a gentle curve to the right but there was nothing to the left. "But there isn't a fork." I said

"That's what we've been telling him." Smith said. "But the damn fool wants to make one."

"Make what?"

"A fork, idiot!"

"Have faith, my boy." Crabtree smiled, showing too many teeth for my taste. "One must have faith!"

The Higgins prototype picked up speed, pushing the dark, muddy water aside like a curtain. Crabtree pushed the engine handle down harder, grinning as he pointed the boat towards a wall of reeds, rocks and trees.

"Hold on to something!" Crabtree said, his voice shaking with excitement. "This might get bumpy!"

Pearl held onto a doorjamb as the boat hit some turbulence. Mr. Smith stood and rode the waves. Thomas pulled out his talismans and ran back to his seat.

I pushed my way inside and shouted over the roar of the engine into Crabtree's ear. "Stop, you fool! The map is wrong! There isn't a fork!"

"But...there should be! Have faith! Ramming speed!"

Crabtree pulled the engine lever completely back and the boat crashed through the reeds, the rocks and knocked over a few young cypress saplings whose seeds had the misfortune of being deposited there. The force knocked both Pearl and I to the floor, head over ass, but Crabtree kept stock still, holding onto the wheel like a pirate of old. He was laughing his head off, enjoying every minute as if it were his last. Unfortunately, if it were, it also would be ours. The boat slammed up and down, like a Hollywood clapboard, on the water. Mr. Smith was knocked out of the wheelhouse. I wrapped myself around Pearl to protect her as we tossed around the cabin like ping pong balls and, surprisingly, she let me.

Three teeth smashing hops later and we suddenly smoothed out. Crabtree pushed the engine back to cruising speed. He turned to us, his smile as wide as ever. "See? I told you there was a fork."

I went to check on the Baskervilles. Thomas had his head in between his knees while Grover was kneeling over the side, vomiting up whatever was left of his breakfast.

Mr. Smith was fuming. "What was that mad fool thinking!"

"He was following the map. And look, he was right. I don't think anyone has been through here in years."

Or it could have been centuries.

Suddenly, Crabtree cried out, "Land ho, boys!"

Thomas and I rushed to the wheelhouse and Pearl met us at the door, flushed and biting her lip. "It's there! He found it!"

Chapter 20

The Guiding Siren

We squeezed passed the wheelhouse to the front of the boat. Thomas whistled and scratched his head. "You don't see that every day."

Greeting us was the waterlogged wooden masthead of a laughing woman frozen forever in a fit of hysteria. The stumps of her arms were still reaching towards the sky although the hands had broken off long ago. On her back was an octopus, holding her around her waist as several of its tentacles gripped her breasts in a tight, fleshy vise. One lone tentacle held a chain where a brass lantern had hung, lighting the way for sailors over 150 years ago.

There, half submerged in the middle of the river, about ten feet away was a scuttled sloop. The tall sails were cut down and all the gun ports were sealed with tar and canvas. Water ran around its eighteen foot long hull as if it were an island so it was free of choking kudzu vines but, as the telltale white splotches witnessed, that did not stop the birds from using it as a perch. I wondered what other fauna nested within the hull.

"It's the *Guiding Siren*. Just like the map said!" Crabtree shouted as he came bouncing towards us. "There she is! She's beautiful! She looks exactly as the drawing in the journal. I knew it! I always knew it!"

"Okay, now that we're here, boss." Thomas said. "Do you want to fill us in on the details now?"

"The *Guiding Siren* is a sloop that Rameau and his men captured late in his career. Normally, pirates would loot and scuttle or, even he is particularly bold, attempt to ransom it back to the owners but the *Guiding Siren* was never heard from again. Everyone just thought he'd scuttled the damn thing and it was lying on the bottom of the Gulf somewhere. However, Rameau makes specific mention of it in the journal and on the map." Crabtree showed us the burned parchment. "See? It's just a circle with the words Guiding Siren. Smith had the brilliant insight that since the ship was taken at the end of his career, Rameau not only scuttled the sloop but also used it as a treasure hold. By this time, he had burned most of his bridges and he knew his time was running out. He needed somewhere to hide his treasures and, well, voila!"

"So, what you are saying is that he sank his piggy bank right here in the swamp?"

"Exactly! Isn't it brilliant?"

Thomas shook his head and spit into the swamp. "It's stupid."

"Think about it, Thomas." I said. "Rameau dammed up this section of the river so he could dry dock the *Guiding Siren* long enough to waterproof it, moor it, fill it full of cargo and then break the dam but put up enough foliage to fool anyone to thinking this branch of the river even existed. He could come back and retrieve his loot whenever he wanted. It's genius."

"Why is it still here, then?"

"Oh, that's the saddest part." Crabtree said. "Rameau was caught up in the Battle of New Orleans and killed. He was never able come back for his treasure."

"His misfortune is our good fortune." Mr. Smith said as he joined us. "Mr. Baskerville, set down anchor."

Thomas looked towards Crabtree who nodded. "Aye, aye, Boss."

"I guess you won't need a digger now." I said to Crabtree.

"Don't be silly, boy. There's more to digging than shoveling. You are our first line."

"First line?"

"I think Crabtree is being polite, Mr. Istenhegyi." Smith said with a toothy smile. "What he means to say is you are fodder."

I didn't waste my breath arguing over Smith's definition of fodder. I soon learned I was to wade through the water, check for booby traps, board the boat, and secure the deck before the rest of the crew came across.

After stripping off my jacket and shirt again, Thomas wrapped the rope around my waist, between my legs, up and over my thighs until it made an extremely uncomfortable harness.

"You've done this before, haven't you?"

"Be quiet or I'll cinch you in places your momma will feel. There. If you go under, at least we'll be able to pull your body back onboard."

"You're a pal. Anyone have any ideas on how I am supposed to get on board?"

"You're clever." Smith said. "I'm sure you'll think of something."

"How about using those portholes?" Thomas said.

"What a brilliant idea!" said Crabtree. "Climb up using those portholes like steps."

"It'll be a snap, Jake. The water has risen since she was scuttled so she's riding low. I bet you could climb up on the first port, toss up a grappling hook, climb up the rope and you're in like Flynn."

"Do we have a grappling hook?"

Thomas smiled brightly, showing a missing lower molar. "Never leave home without one."

I wondered exactly how athletic my new company imagined I was. "I don't know. Why can't we pull up anchor and get closer?"

"Boobytraps." Mr. Smith said.

"So you need me to go and trip a few as I shuffle across a rushing river. How deep is it, anyway? What if I don't touch bottom?"

"The Higgins prototype was built for shallows, my boy." Crabtree patted me on my shoulder. "I doubt it will go much higher than your chin."

"Do you have a plank I can walk across or am I expected to jump in and wade?"

"For chrissakes, Jake, stop burning sunlight and get on with it." Thomas said. "We could all learn to walk on water by the time you get going."

"But what about-"

"Just get on with it!" Smith snapped.

"Aye, aye, Boss."

I swung my legs over and eased down slowly into the water. It was cold and made certain unmentionables very, very uncomfortable.

"How's that harness holding up?"

"I'm losing the feeling in my ass."

"What ass?"

"Go to hell, Thomas."

It was up to my armpits by the time my feet hit bottom.

"Sweet Jesus, it's deep."

Thomas handed me a machete and a coil of rope attached to a small grappling hook. "Try not to step on any gators. They hate that."

I gave Thomas the appropriate one finger salute and waded slowly over to the Rameau's pirate ship. The mud sucked at my boots each step. The boodaddy pouch floated and splashed wretched swamp water in my face. I was getting colder with every step and –wait! Did something just touch my leg?

"Hey, Jake!" Thomas yelled. "You can swim, right?"

"Yes, ugh…why?" I asked as I struggled to pull up my boot without losing it.

"I just remembered my granddaddy telling me stories about losing fellas out in the swamps to sinkho-"

Just then the muck beneath my feet shifted, there was a great KABLOOSH and the water swallowed me up. Instinctively, I closed my eyes and held my breath as sour, stale swamp water ran up my nose and into my ears. I felt a tug from the rope harness and then release. What? Why didn't Thomas pull me out? I wrapped the rope around my arm, keeping a firm grasp on the grappling hook, and yanked it only to find it completely slack. I fought back the anger and frustration as I wrestled against the sucking mud and lost a boot in the process. My legs were cramping from the cold and exhaustion and my lungs were burning, craving oxygen. Claustrophobic panic began clawing at me. The need to breathe, the gripping fear of crushing water pulling me down gave me an adrenaline rush to free myself and push upwards. My hands flailed, desperate to grab onto anything and I brushed against something. I opened my eyes in time to see blood orange teeth coming at my face. It was a rat and I had it by the tail. It gnashed its teeth and I swung out with the machete, cutting at the creature in half. I dropped the machete and let it fall away as I pushed towards light.

I broke the surface, sputtering and gagging. I heard splashing coming from the shore. The water was turning red with blood. Basically, a dinner bell for gators and God only knew what else. The terror gave me the adrenaline boost I needed and I made it to the sloop, scrambled up the side and was standing on a ledge of a porthole. My cold fingers turning white as I held onto the wood with a death grip.

Chapter 21

Onboard

The ledge was five inches deep and the porthole was uncomfortably cramped. The tar and wood plug that Rameau's men had used in the porthole was weakening and I kicked it in easily. There was a splash and skittering, clawing sounds when it landed. It was too dark inside to see what made the noises, but I could make a very educated guess.

I swung the grappling hook and tossed it over the gunwale where it hung firm. I took a deep breath and climbed up the rope, the rough texture burning my hands with each grip. Once I reached the gunwale, I pulled myself up, flopped onto the deck and lay there, gasping and waited for the machine gun thumping of my heart to settle down.

I fumbled with the rope harness until I finally undid the knot. I sat up, pulled it off and looked at the end of the rope. It was frayed as if something had cut through it.

"Istenhegyi!" Smith called out to me.

"Just give me a minute to catch my breath." I stood up and waved the frayed end to the only man on deck. "I'm here no thanks to...where are Thomas and Mr. Crabtree?"

"In the wheelhouse with Pearl."

"Oh, still…what the hell happened to the rope?"

"I have no idea." Smith shrugged. "Where is your machete?"

"I dropped it after I was attacked by a damned giant rat!"

"Pity. Perhaps you cut the rope? It doesn't matter now. Now, go find the hatch and see what is in the hold."

"But-"

Smith dismissed me with barely a flip of his hand as he made his way to the wheelhouse.

Okay, so where was the hatch? There wasn't much other than bits of tree limbs, dirt and leaves that littered the deck. The posts that held the sails were sawed down to stubs that jutted up like broken teeth. The wood felt dangerously spongy in some places and completely missing in others. It's a miracle I didn't crash through to the hell when I first landed. I walked awkwardly across the deck since my booted foot felt ten pounds heavier than my other. I took the boot off and tossed it overboard; I'd beg Radu's forgiveness later.

"Okay, Janos…find the hatch." I muttered as I wandered across the deck. "Hatch, hatch…if I were a hatch where would I….ow, dammit!" I stubbed my toe on a thick, metal loop in the middle of a square door. "Well, that looks promising."

I grabbed the metal loop with both hands and pulled. It wouldn't budge an inch. I took a deep breath, bent at the knees, and groaned as I pulled even harder. This time the hatch gave way, the warped wood groaning in protest as it opened.

The sunlight only pierced the darkness enough to show me a staircase that led down into the hold. I picked up a stick and threw it into the dark. There was a splash like before and that same clawing, skittering sound.

I could hear the engine of the *Precipice* as it got closer.

One guess on whose job it would be to go down into the Big Dark Scary Hole?

The boodaddy in the leather pouch hanging from my neck grew hot and started twitching, as if something were inside. I squeezed the pouch and the quivering stopped. That was weird. It had never done that before now. What exactly was down there in the dark to get it so agitated? I sat cross legged on the deck and considered my options.

On one hand, the ship's hull was leaking. The river was wide but not all that deep. That didn't worry me so much.

On the other, slightly more dangerous hand, the hull was inhabited by orange fanged giant rats. My machete was at the bottom of the river and I was currently shirtless and barefoot. The only thing between me and whatever lurked down there were a pair of waterlogged pants and a leather pouch around my neck.

Perfect.

There was a clunk as the *Precipice* brushed alongside the *Guiding Siren*. Soon after that, two metallic hooks latched onto the gunwale and I could hear the clickety clack of a ladder unfolding down the side.

Still, it could be worse. Thomas and Grover would be here soon as back up. They would have weapons, surely. Or at least a flashlight. With their help, what were a dozen giant rats? Nothing! We'd get rid of them, haul up whatever treasure we find down there and be home for supper.

My mood brightened at the thought. I wasn't alone, for a change. I had to remember that.

I got to my feet. "Finally joining the party, Thomas? I thought I was going to have to drag all the treasure out myself, you lazy bastard. Hurry up!"

A bald head appeared to reveal a smiling Mr. Smith. "I hope I'm invited to the party."

"I assumed you were Thomas."

"As often is the problem of the slow witted."

Mr. Smith moved with grace despite his bulk and made it to the deck with little trouble. He smoothed down his linen suit, gave his purple pouch a pat before reaching over to help Pearl come aboard. She carried a heavy backpack that she shrugged off as soon as she stepped on the deck.

"What about the rest of ...ahhh damn!" A sharp pain in my chest from the pouch made me wince.

Smith pulled out a .45 Colt and pointed it at me. "They aren't coming."

Chapter 22

The Purple Velvet Bag

"I was wondering when you'd show your true face." I said, showing more bravado than I felt with a gun pointed at my chest. "You weren't all that slick, pal. I knew you were following me. I have pictures of you back on Canal Street. So, why don't you just drop the charade?"

"Charade? You flatter yourself. We came here with only the best intentions. I have a buyer lined up in Europe and I could make a nice fortune if I delivered the Cross of Trismegitus. But then we learned that you were also in New Orleans." He said my name as if it hurt his teeth. "Jake Istenhegyi. I'm sure even you can see the wisdom in the adage of two birds, one stone.

"Was it worth killing James to get to me on board the treasure hunt train?"

"We were one man too heavy and James was the weakest link. Looking back, perhaps the compulsion spell I seeded the paper with was unnecessary. I should've given my niece's charms more credit."

Pearl shrank at her uncle's words.

"So, now you have me. Well done. Bravo. So, what do you want? By the gun in your hand, I can't believe it's anything good for my health. Why go through all this? Why didn't you just kill me?"

"We have other plans for you." Smith grimaced and dug the palm of his free hand into his forehead as if trying to erase a headache. "Shhh, shhh….stop screaming. I hear you." He glared at me with bloodshot eyes. "I admit, killing you was an important piece of the ritual, but you wouldn't stay dead."

I kept my poker face tied on with frayed strings.

"What are you talking about? Dead? That's crazy. I think I'd know if I were dead. Pearl, what is he talking about?"

Pearl shook her head and stared at the deck.

"Don't ask her. She's an idiot child. Her only worth is as a vessel for a great power. But what would you know about power? Give me that piece of trash." He grabbed the pouch and yanked it off, snapping the leather cord. "Crabtree's back alley hoodoo is a slap in the face of true power." He threw it with such force it landed on the bank in a thick batch of kudzu.

"Let me show you true power, Istenhegyi, and you can ask her why you deserve to die."

Smith unlatched the purple velvet pouch from his belt and put it into Pearl's outstretched hands. She opened it with trembling fingers, pulling the velvet down to reveal a mass of dark wavy hair stitched to what looked like a peeled apple, brown and dried out. My breath caught in my throat as I realized...it was a head. A shrunken head.

"Ma petite mama...shhh, shhh...ma belle fille." he cooed, over this grotesque, shriveled lump and kissed it gently on the stitches that held shut the eyes. "Oui, ma petite mama. I have him. See?" The thick threads weaved through the eyelids quivered as ....oh God...the eyelids were trying to open. And the lips...*Istenhem!* The bloated, pouty lips trembled and cracked as a thin, desiccated slip of a tongue peeked out. The tip was split into two and they flickered like a snake's as it tasted the air. "Oui, it is him. As I promised."

My façade cracked as I gasped. "What the *hell is that?*"

"Show respect! Don't you recognize her? No? What a shame. She remembers you. She screams your name constantly. She cries to us, her children, in our dreams. She screams in pain, in agony, for justice. Ma petite mama. She fills my head with your name."

That long black, wavy hair. No, no. Surely, it burned off the fire. No, it was impossible.

"Harleaux?" I whispered. "Henrietta Harleaux?"

The lips on the head peeled back into a grimace and a garbled word hissed out, dry and hot. *"Issshhhheeegyyyyiiii!"*

Pearl's eyes glazed over, her shoulders slumped and she started panting heavily. The head toppled from her hand and Smith deftly caught it before it hit the deck, snatching up the head.

"No…Grandmere…I can't…I won't!"

"Let go, girl!" Smith slapped Pearl across the face.

"No!"

"Obey your Grandmere!"

She fell to the ground, convulsing, and her face twisted as she shrieked in pain. Foam dribbled down her chin and she shuddered once more violently and then stopped. She lay there on the wooden, soft deck still as death.

I started to rush towards her, but Smith pulled the hammer back on the Colt.

"Stay there, Istenhegyi."

"She's dying." I yelled. "Help her!"

"I don't need any man's help." Pearl pushed herself up to her knees and sat down. She wiped the foam from her chin and flicked it away in disgust. "She's getting more disrespectful, Theo.   That bastard child, that's her only anchor...why haven't you disposed of it yet?"

"She has hidden him, Mama."

"Clever bitch." Pearl got to her feet and stretched. She smiled as she luxuriated in the movement. "Still, it is only a matter of time. Ugh, hide that ugly thing." she said, waving a hand at the shrunken head in Smith's hands.

"Yes, Mama." He stashed it back in the pouch and clipped it on his belt.

She bit her lip and locked her eyes on me. It was *her*. That fierce wild cat I remembered.

"Hello there, lover. Miss me?"

Memories of Friday night flooded me, but Pearl's face was replaced with the lumpish face of the shrunken head. My throat convulsed and bit back the bile. I shook my head to wipe away the sight. The reality hit me in the gut. "You? What did you...why did you?"

She laughed. It was the same melodic laugh I remember from the first time we met; back in the barn, over Bear's eviscerated body. "Look at him! He's adorable. So, confused. He really isn't all that bright, is he? Still, he has a few talents that I enjoyed using."

I steadied my face and spoke through clenched teeth. "I'm sorry to say that I don't remember very much. The weekend is a bit of a blur. What happened?"

"That's something I'd like to know too, lover. When we left you, you were quite dead. Theo was very thorough; he slit your throat and bled you in accordance to the ritual. I cut out your heart and carved the sigils on your chest myself."

The strange black marks on my chest that washed away in the shower. The pain in my throat, all that blood. Christ! That's why Saturday was missing. I was dead. It takes time to build a new heart and fill a body with blood.

"I knew something was wrong when Theo sent me back inside my skull and your soul wasn't there, locked in with me. I was so very disappointed. We could've had so much more fun. It gets so lonely in there."

She started walking towards me, her hips rolling seductively with each step.

"Tell me your secret, love. How did you do it? Why aren't you dead?"

I shrugged. "Clean living?"

"Oh, my handsome boy." She stroked my face. The smell of jasmine swirled around me and my head started buzzing. "You aren't that clean. I can still taste you." Her fingers combed through my hair, softly, on both sides until her hands clasped my head. She kissed me, hard. My breath caught it my throat as her tongue rolled and tickled every inch inside my mouth

Damn. I felt that betraying heat growing down deep inside me. My eyelids fluttered as the heat flooded me, roaring up through my veins, scorching my brain. I wanted to grab her and tear into her. This wasn't a gesture of love, no. I felt no soft sentiment towards this woman. I wanted to devour her, to tear into her, feel her completely. My mind felt blank. Rational thought was a fading blur as the only thing that was real was the gnawing need to engorge myself on this woman. *No! This is wrong! Stop!* My hands clenched into fists and I bit my lip until salty blood trickled into my mouth. *"No."* Just saying the word made the red flood pull back, clearing my head. I opened my eyes, pushed her away and took a step away from her. ***"No."***

"Damn." She smirked and looked surprised. "Well, aren't you just a box of surprises. Not even a twitch?" She grabbed at my crotch and smiled slyly at my body's betrayal. "Pity. Oh well, so be it. You made your choice. Theo?"

The big man snapped to attention at her voice. Suddenly, I saw him for what he was: a thin, stick puppet masked inside a mountain of flesh whose strings were pulled by a hellwitch of a mother. I wish I could feel sorry for the bastard but it's kind of hard after learning he'd killed me two nights before. That sort of information tends to color my compassion.

"It's time to put our digger to work."

Chapter 23

X Marks the Spot

I looked down into the dark, scary hole.

Guess who is going down first? If you guessed the poor bastard standing, shirtless, shoeless with the barrel of a revolver stabbing him in the back, pat yourself on the back.

"After you?" I flashed my brightest smile at Smith.

He did not return my smile nor laugh at my attempt at humor.

"A guy had to try, right?"

Smith tapped the gun into my back. "Get moving, Istenhegyi."

Down below in the hull, the treasure of the Pirate Rameau, moldering in rotted wooden crates, stacks of gold, silver and piles of precious jewels were waiting for someone brave enough to take the first steps down this ladder and claim them. Someone who wasn't afraid of giant rats with orange teeth that nested there or someone who perhaps was more dressed for the occasion, say, someone with waterproof boots or even a goddamn shirt, for crying out loud. Not to mention someone who had a weapon of some sort. A gun, or a knife or, hell, even a sharpened stick right now would make me feel a lot braver about climbing down into the dark, scary hole.

"How about some light?"

"When you get to the bottom, I'll throw you a flashlight. Don't drop it."

"You're a pal."

There were steps that led down below. I could see four of them with more below. They looked sturdy and thick with little water damage.

"I hope you don't mind if I talk." I said as I started down the steps. "I ramble when I'm nervous so feel free to ignore me."

I felt each step with my bare foot before trusting it with my full weight. I counted them as I went down. The first four were dry but by the sixth one, the damp was settling in and the wood was warping. When I stepped off the final eighth step, I was in ankle deep water.

"Okay! I'm here!" I shouted to Smith. Around me I could hear splashing and skittering of things in the water. "Smith! Goddammit, throw me a flashlight! There's something down here!"

"For a man who can't stay dead, what are a few rats?" Smith said as he tossed the flashlight down.

I caught it and turned on the light. "If you're so brave, you come down here."

He laughed. "And ruin my fine Italian loafers?"

"You wouldn't happen to have a spare pair to share, would you? This water is damn cold."

He didn't respond and I walked slowly through the murky water, keeping within the thin, wispy circle of light. My teeth chattered against the cold. I tried to control my breathing. Breathing through my nose assaulted my senses with mold and decay but breathing through my mouth was just a different sort of torture.

The flashlight put out a feeble glow that barely illuminated a foot around me. I couldn't make out exactly the dimensions of the hull. I shined the light up to the roof. It was only a few inches taller than me. Great. I pushed aside the claustrophobia. I shined the light around me hoping to scare off anything that might prefer the dark. It worked as I could hear more splashes and chittering as things ran away from me.

In the shadows, I could see lopsided square shapes along the walls on both sides of me. Waterlogged crates? Not exactly the ornate treasure chests I'd seen in storybooks as a child. It was a bit of a disappointment.

"Hey, I can see something glittering in the water. Do you mind if I take some gold coins for my troubles?" I asked.

"Take whatever you want, Istenhegyi, load down your pockets. You'll sink faster that way."

I dropped the coin. "So, tell a dead man your story. Amuse me while I wander around in the dark."

"I'm not here to entertain you. Just to make sure you do your job."

"I hear you. Big man with a gun watching over the little guy with no shoes on. Story of the world, isn't it? But, I'm nervous and, like I said, I ramble when I'm scared so...be grateful I am at least speaking in English. Do you speak Hungarian? Don't answer that. Of course, you don't. Nobody outside Hungary does. Why would they? Did you know it is one of the hardest languages to learn? It is- ahh!" I stepped on something soft and I stopped moving, stopped breathing...I think even my heart stopped beating. The soft thing didn't bite so I reached into the water and pulled out a swath of wet velvet. I threw it to the side and started breathing again.

"Did you find something?"

"No, false alarm. So, I'm guessing your name isn't really Smith, is it? A little cliché, don't you think?"

"Cliches are cliché because they work."

"Has he found it yet?" Harleaux snapped.

"No." Smith let out a bored sigh.

"Why not? It's not that big a hull, even that idiot Grover would have found it by now."

"It would help if this flashlight was more than a candle with batteries and if I knew what the hell I was looking for." I shouted back at her. "There's nothing down here but stink, filth, rats and broken crates."

"Then check the crates, idiot!"

"Which one, your Royal Bitchness? There are hundreds down here. What did you expect? It would have a big red X painted on it or a label that reads 'Cross of Trimegitus, Salt of Eternal Life - This End Up'?"

"You insufferable Gypsy piece of…give me that gun! Give it to me!"

I heard a scuffle above and the familiar sound of gunfire as two shots whizzed by me and plunked into the water. I didn't give her another chance to get a better aim and I hustled farther away and out of her sight of range. There, in the farthest part of the hull, I found a tall wooden box and hid behind it. In the weak light, I could see it was made of a dark wood, something heavy like mahogany, and was completely intact. There was even a large golden plaque on the front that read, CRUCEM TRISMEGITUS, SAL VITAE AETERNAE.

Below that was a label that hung loosely by one corner. I smoothed it out to read, THIS END UP.

"Well….son of a bitch."

There was a golden latch that held the doors closed. I unlatched it and they swung open to reveal a velvet lined reliquary. It was like a miniature shrine with golden cherubs that held a cracked stained-glass box. Inside the box was a 9 x 12-inch wooden cross with gold inlays and jewels that surrounded a secondary smaller one, the sapphire Cross of Trismegitus. Remarkably, the Baskervilles had made a nice duplicate considering all they had to work from was a sketch in the journal.

Inside the sapphire cross, an orb that held a small crystal shard.

I smashed the stained glass with my flashlight and removed the Cross. It was heavy, around five pounds. I rubbed the crystal that covered the Salt with my finger and I felt an electric spark. My heartbeat raced and a peculiar fire in my blood told me it was the Salt. It called to its sister fragments in my blood.

Hope soared through me. I had found it! Yes! I could avoid Giovanna's fate and live...good God, I could live forever.

Eternal life. I'd never really thought about it.

Suddenly, there was a splash and then the sound of more splashing. One of them had ventured down and was running towards me. By the sound, I suspected Harleaux.

Then there was heavier splashing. Smith running after Harleaux.

"Mother, stop, please...stop!"

"No!"

"Mother, we don't have any light. It's dark as night. You're going to hurt yourself."

Damn! They could have the Cross but I not the Salt. I hit the crystal casing with my flashlight but the metal canister just bounced off. I looked for something heavier. Nothing! I tried to pry the crystal out of the cross but, no! It was wedged in there too tightly. I'd need a chisel or a knife. Damn!

They were seconds from finding me even in the pitch dark. I needed a way out. What did Bear always say? Never get yourself trapped, kid. Always, always, ALWAYS have a way out! I could hear him now. Well,

I'm sorry, Bear, but I doubt you had ever been trapped in the belly of a scuttled pirate ship.

I heard more splashing but this time it came from behind me. I spun the light towards the sound. It was one of those giant rats. It dropped in from a hole in the roof. Yes! You beautiful, plague ridden, orange tooth bastard! A way out. If I could just make it over there without being noticed, knock over a crate and climb up to the roof and make it up to the deck. I'd be home free. I waded towards a crate and quickly lowered it beneath the hole. It was the perfect size. I slid the Cross into my belt and climbed on top.

"Come out, you bastard!" Harleaux shouted. "Come out now or…"

I bit my tongue from asking *or what?* and kept focused on climbing out as quickly as I could while the darkness hid me.

"I'll shoot her. Pearl. I'll shoot her right in the head."

I stopped. "What?" *Damn.*

"You're not the only one with an immortality trick. I'll just pop back into my skull. I have other granddaughters, better granddaughters who are more beautiful and better hosts."

I heard her pull the hammer back. "She has a little boy waiting for her, if that makes any difference."

Shit Shit Shit SHIT!

I climbed down and stepped out from behind the case.

"Good choice." She said as she blinded me with her flashlight. "What is that in your belt? Put your hands up, Istenhegyi."

Damn. I held up my hands.

"You found it and weren't going to share? That is very rude. Theo, if you please."

Theo took a sloshed through the water and tugged the Cross from my belt.

"Sorry about your shoes." I said.

"I can't tell if you are clever or simply stupid."

"The jury is out on both counts."

He shook his head sadly before going back to his mother.

"Now, get down on your knees, Istenhegyi."

I did as I was told and she pressed the gun against my forehead.

"A bullet to the brain? You slit my throat, bled me dry and cut out of my heart last time. A bit anticlimactic, don't you think?"

She dug the barrel into my skin. "I don't know what the hell you are, Istenhegyi. I doubt this will even kill you but I bet a bullet to the brain will shut you up long enough to dump your body into the swamp. I wonder how long do you think it'll take you to resurrect inside an alligator's stomach?"

A very dark terror gripped inside my gut. In one of Bear's beloved pulp magazines, the scene would read something more dramatic like, 'I bent down like a chump on his way to propose while the dame with murder in her eyes kissed my forehead with the steel barrel of her .45 pistol.' But the truth is, I'm a stupid man who stumbled into immortality and now I was going to end up a pile of alligator shit in a goddamn Louisiana swamp. How was that for irony? I was laughing. It came out a bit muffled but, trust me, inside I was howling.

"Look up at me, lover. Oh, yes, that's it." Harleaux smiled wide, showing all her teeth. "That's the look I want to remember." she said as she pulled the trigger.

Chapter 24

Friends in Low Places

Click.

I wince at the flat sound, momentarily stunned by the lack of pain and the blackness that I imagine usually follows being shot in the head.

Click, CLICK, CLICK!

"Dammit!" She throws the gun at me and it bounces painfully off my shoulder.

"Now, that's a disappointment, right there, that is." There is a new halo of light from a flashlight. It is Thomas. He glides over, barely making a ripple in the water. One eye is swollen shut and there is blood trailing down from his scalp. "A typical rube move. Not checking the chambers." He pulls back the hammer on my revolver. "You can make damn sure I did not make that mistake. Hello, Jake. Having trouble?'

"A fair amount, yes." I stand and wade over to Thomas. "Smith has the Cross."

"So I saw. I was able to hide most of my footsteps in all their splashing around. Give the Cross to Jake, Mr. Smith." He points the gun for emphasis. "Please."

I take the Cross and Thomas motions for me to put it in his satchel. I lay it on top of the fake one.

"Well, this has been fun." Thomas says as he walks slowly backwards towards the stairs. "Always good doing business with out of towners. I hope you enjoy the rest of your stay here in New Orleans."

"You're going to leave us here?" the woman wearing Pearl's face says. "That's inhuman!"

"You're right. Where are my manners?" Thomas swerves his gun hand towards Smith. "This is for Grover, you son of a bitch." And pulls the trigger.

Smith falls backwards, a red pool pillows around his head.

"No!" Harleaux screams and lunges for the purple pouch on Smith's belt. She tears it off, tucks it into her chest and folds herself over it.

"Stop her! Grab the skull!" I shout but it is too late. Pearl stares back us with wide lost eyes. In her hands she cradles the head of her grandmother, the bitch, Henrietta Harleaux.

"What is happening? Where am I?" She sees the floating body of her uncle next to her and gasps. Her breath heaves in and out as if she has never tasted air before. And then she screams.

Thomas raises the revolver towards her.

"No, Thomas. Not her."

"She's just as much as part of this as he is. She killed Crabtree. She damn near killed me." He pulls the hammer back. "She has to pay."

"You don't understand. It's not her. She's not-"

Just then a terrible thump rattles the deck overhead. Splinters of wood rain down and the rats, all the rats run away through hidden holes.

"What the hell is that? Did a tree fall on the boat?"

In a blind panic, Pearl stands and runs, pushing through us and towards the only source of light: the stairwell.

"That bitch!" Thomas turns to take aim but I grab his arm and jerk it up just as he pulls the trigger. The bullet lodges harmlessly in the wood above us.

"Stop!" I shout into his face, twisting the gun out of his hand. "She's not the one responsible."

"Oh, yeah? Then who did I see smashing in Crabtree's head? Her twin?"

I point at the leather pouch that Pearl clutches to her chest. "The skull!"

"The what?"

Pearl stops at the stairs and looks at me with beautiful, black doe eyes, wet with tears.

"Pearl, drop the pouch." I tell her. "Drop it."

She shakes her head. "But she is my-"

Her words are cut off as a roar comes down from above as a thick, green leafy wave rushes down and wraps itself around Pearl. She screams and fights but it overwhelms her and yanks her up to the deck, slamming her body mercilessly on the steps.

"Follow me!" I run towards the stairs. Thomas, to his credit, is right on my heels.

We crawl out on deck to a nightmare. A towering ramshackle creature is there, made up of a jigsaw of kudzu, moss, sticks and mud. It roars a bubbling, raspy roar like a pipe spitting out a mildewy clog.

It holds Pearl high in the air. Her head is thrown back and her mouth is agape in a silent scream. She is suspended between two tendrils, her arms and legs are stretched as it tears her slowly apart.

Thomas drops his satchel and crosses himself. "Sweet Mother of Christ, it is the Honey Island Swamp Monster. Shoot it!"

I notice a white spot in the center of its chest. It is an oyster shell. There are leather drawstrings intertwined in the leaves.

I touch my chest and wonder…

"Boodaddies are protective spirits, right?"

"What the hell are you talking about? We don't have time for none of that nonsense. Shoot it!"

"I wonder…..Boodaddy! Hey! Boodaddy! It's me, Jake!" I pound my chest where the pouch had hung.

It stops roaring and looks down at me.

"I'll be damned." Thomas says. "It's listening to you."

"You are mine," I yell at the creature. "Obey me! Let her go."

The Boodaddy releases its grip and Pearl falls to the deck in a crushing thump.

I grimace. "Ouch."

"Ooooof. Better watch your phrasing, Jake."

I go to Pearl. She is unconscious and in a fetal position, protectively curled around that horrible skull. I don't see anything broken, no blood. I hold her wrist and feel for her pulse. There is a weak fluttering and then nothing. "No!" I grind my teeth and check again, feeling for any sign of life. Wait, there is something. A slight pulse that grows stronger.

I tear the pouch away from her clutching fingers. I reach in, snag the skull with my fingers inside its eye sockets and pull it out.

"Thomas, take Pearl back to the *Precipice*. I'll meet you there after I get rid of this."

"I hope you know what you're doing, Jake."

"Me too."

Thomas picks up the unconscious Pearl and I watch them carefully get back to the *Precipice*.

I look up at the Boodaddy. It stands there and waits for my instructions. I hold up the skull and shout, "Take it far away and destroy it. Grind it into dust."

I toss the skull into the air and a whip made of kudzu, sticks and mud snatches it out of the air and pulls it into the depths of its mossy chest. It shivers all its leaves in acknowledgment, collapses into a pile and swirls into a green, a shrieking whirlwind of leaves, sticks and mud. It hops off the ship and skips across the water like a stone until it hits the bank and the rolls into the deep underbrush, disappearing into it or, more truthfully, becoming a part of the land.

"It's good to have friends in low places, don't you think, Thomas?"

I turn to my friend, but he is gone.

So is Pearl.

And so is the satchel.

I hear the motor of the *Precipice* in the distance.

It is going to be a long, long, long walk home.

Chapter 25

Lucky Breaks and Full Pockets

I caught a lucky break when Paul came looking for us when the *Precipice* didn't return on time. He found me just as I made it out into the main stretch of the river and gave him a ride back to port. No questions asked. I understood why Crabtree paid him so well. A man who asked no questions was a good man to employ.

I stood on the deck and watched as the sun began to hang heavy in the sky. I was cold to the bone. Paul loaned me a shirt, a pair of socks and some rubber boots but the cold I was feeling was more than the winter air biting at me. I was counting all the things I'd lost today and, with each tick, my temperature dropped. My wallet with the only picture I had ever had of my mother. Bear's copy of *Black Mask* which he was going to be sore as hell at me for losing provided he ever returned. My mother's amulet. They were all in my jacket that Smith was so adamant that I remove. Now, I could see it was an attempt to separate me from the boodaddy. He didn't know I wore it around my neck and not stashed in my pocket.

Worst of all, I lost the Salt. I had it...right in my hand. I had it! I pounded my fist in frustration. So....close.

I watched the sun go down. It looked like it was slowly drowning in the dark bayou. I did my best not to let my mood follow it into the dark depths. The weight of the gold coins in my pockets helped, if only a little.

Chapter 26

Silver Tongued Devil

It was late evening and streetlights splashed pools of creamy white light onto the sidewalk outside the Odyssey Shop.

At her counter, Mama Effie and Radu were huddled over a magazine, deep in conversation. She raised an eyebrow at me but didn't ask any questions.

"Look what the rat dragged in!" Radu said, smiling.

"Cat, dear." Mama Effie corrected him. "However, by the smell you're bringing in here, it could be. You reek, boy!"

"Sorry about that. I just spent a day in the swamp fighting for my life. Thanks for asking." I pointed a finger at my brother. "What are you doing here? You're not supposed to be here at all, Radu."

"Plans changed." He explained with his patented Hollywood matinee smile. "Wait. Those aren't my boots. Where are my boots? And my jacket? What happened to my clothes?"

"Eaten by gators. I'll take it out of your rent."

"But I don't pay-"

"Exactly. Would you like to start?" Radu pursed his lips and went back to his magazine. "You're here late, Mama Effie."

"You missed an entire day, *Boss.*" She said, turning a page. "I'd say you were the late one."

I was too tired to rattle sabers with her tonight. "I'm going to bed. Good night."

"Wait a minute, boy!" she said. "I didn't stay here for my health. I've got something I need to say."

My shoulders slumped with exhaustion. "Fine, just make it quick."

"First off, things are squared with Brannigan. I'm not saying you're going to be invited to be the Grand Marshall of the St. Patrick's Day parade any time soon but, as far as to the business of Mallone's money, it's done."

"Good."

"But I'm still very upset with you."

"Oh, God, what now?"

She tapped Radu on the shoulder. "Why the hell did they send a fusspot like you and leave someone so charming and pleasant like this one in the wings?"

"Because he's not an Istenhegyi."

"Aaaand that explains everything." Radu said under his breath.

Mama Effie laughed and clapped her hands. With joy! I had never seen her laugh out of happiness. Out of spite, yes, but never had I seen her laugh in such good humor. It was frightening.

"I love this boy! He is so interesting." Her voice was light but there was something in her eyes that was dark and sharp. "Your brother has been telling me the most interesting *stories* all day."

Ah. And the snake was back in the Garden. I shot Radu a look.

"Look at the time! I still have packing to do." Radu gathered up his magazine and excused himself.

"I wouldn't believe everything you hear, Mama Effie. You know what they say. Gypsies are storytellers. Silver tongued devils, the lot of them."

"Oh, really?" She leaned forward, balancing her chin on the tips of her fingertips. I knew that look. That was the one she looked when she was sizing up her newest opponent. My mouth went dry.

"Did he tell you his plans of going to Hollywood? Making it big as a movie star?"

"Yes. Did you know he can sing and dance? Also he plays several instruments. An incredibly talented boy.

We were discussing names that would look best on a marquee."

"Oh really? Well, who knows?" A nervous laugh bubbled out of me and I hated myself a little for it. "Maybe that silver tongue devil will find his fortune out west."

"We can only hope for the best." She shrugged as she left her throne. "Well, Boss, I've dawdled here too long as it is. Good night. I'll see you in the morning."

"Yes, good night, see you tomorrow."

She opened the door and stood there for a second. "Don't worry. I'll lock up the shop. I'd hate for any *kisértet* to find their way in."

The door slammed and I exhaled a breath I didn't know I'd been holding.

DAMN.

The End

The Adventure Continues!!
Volume 2

*Fished-Eyed Men, Fedoras, and Steel-Toed Pumps

*Road Trips Acid Baths and One-Eyed Bastards

*Corpses, Coins, Ghosts and Goodbyes

ABOUT THE AUTHOR

Nikki Nelson-Hicks lives in with five cats, two dogs, two spawn and one husband.

It's a weirdly quiet home.

Made in the USA
Monee, IL
12 September 2020

42247213R10187